GLOSSOLALIA

Glossolalia:

Psychological Suspense

TANTRA BENSKO

ISBN: 0692551522

ISBN 13: 978-0692551523

IB
Insubordinate Books
Berkeley, CA
2016

http://www.insubordinatebooks.com/

Table of Contents

CHAPTER ONE
Chemical XXX

What was the sound outside D-CIDE's office window? Clinks and bangs. One boom was so loud Nancy clasped her pale, slender hands over her ears. Tuning things out was her superpower.

"Have any plans for the weekend?" the tall secretary, Martha, loudly asked her, leaning over her desk in the office, as she grabbed a floating hair lit up by the evening sun. Martha elaborately waved her hands in front of Nancy's face as she did so.

Nancy got confused by the motion and forgot what she'd been thinking about. Oh yes, the weekend. It was Friday already. "Fighting." Nancy spoke with her head high and her shoulders back, her rosy cheeks plumped with a confident smile.

D-CIDE'S saleswoman, Betsy, looked Nancy up and down and said, "What, shadow boxing?"

Nancy laughed and said, "You know, uncle Geoff told me I was so upset by my shadow when I first noticed it, I pounded my fists on the sidewalk trying to beat it up." (Geoff was pronounced like Joff.) "He said I didn't know my own strength. And that's when he first decided I should

1

have fighting lessons. Been studying ever since." She chuckled, "And fighting off my shadow, too!"

"Who's winning?" chirped Betsy, grinning. "Honey, if you could team up with your shadow and fight together, I'll bet you'd be able to take us all on at the same time."

"I'd never have pictured you as a brawler, Nancy-Pants. More like a fashion model." Martha teased her dyed blond hair with an ivory comb as she spoke, her overdone make-up doing a poor job of offsetting her overweight condition, though she was obviously using deep shadow to make her elderly cheeks look hollow. "A little slip of a thing like you. You selling tickets? I gotta see that."

"Karate tournament tomorrow." Nancy pumped her small fist toughened by calluses. "It's going to be fun."

Meanwhile, Betsy, passing by Nancy's desk, glanced down at the cat calendar lying on it and chuckled, pointing to that day's square sitting at the beginning of February: a calico playing the piano with an orchestra behind it was the featured image. "What's this? Do you see one guy some days, another guy on other days, and both on the other days? Looks like a doozy tonight, then, eh? Double triangle day!"

"What do you mean?" asked Nancy, her lusciously full pink lips angling slightly sideways in bewilderment.

Betsy answered: "The blue triangular marks on those days on your calendar. Some turned up, some facing down, and others superimposing an upward and a downward one. Woo hoo, girl!"

Nancy looked at the calendar where Betsy had pointed but didn't notice the marks. Nancy stared, straining her eyes trying to find anything like that on the paper. She decided they must be blue. The sky seemed pale gray to her like a diluted shadow spread thin. *Is something wrong with my color vision?*

"I don't doubt that our Miss Nancy's got plenty of men clamoring for her," said Betsy, chortling, as her oversized glasses slid down her nose. "Just look at that perfect little body!" Betsy held in her stomach, stuck out her bust, widened her eyes and plumped her lips while prancing past.

Nancy decided her officemates must be pranking her, and she stuck out her tongue. "OK, then, I'll take you all on! Take that!" Her eyes glistened, as she stood up and took a classic position of karate readiness. The manager and Betsy assumed the position too, and they all leaped about, hands flattened and poised as if prepared to strike. They all competed for having the most faux-fierce looks.

"It's got to be fun being ageless. I want to know your secret." Martha pulled the belt on her bright yellow dress down over her substantial hips, panting.

Nancy maintained her smile, but she felt bad the women were apparently judging their appearance in comparison to hers. She pulled a hair tie out of her desk drawer and pulled her strawberry blondness back to a less attractive style.

"We *all* want to know your secret," offered Betsy. She put her hands on her hips and stared, eyes bugged out.

"Fighting's a good way to deal with the awful tedium of working here?" asked Martha, tapping out the grimy ashtray into the waste basket. Some of the ashes spilled and she ground them into the dark carpet, turning it a nauseating gray.

"Pretty much, yes. And it's fun. Besides, it's only part time." Nancy didn't mention having defense tactics in her subconscious could come in handy if she sleepwalked someplace dangerous during one of her annoying amnesiac bouts.

Betsy asked, "Why don't you look for a job elsewhere if you don't like it? Really, why stay at D-CIDE when everyone knows how you feel about the environment? It can't be

3

because you find your uncle irresistibly charming." She pulled her face back into her neck and pulled her lips back into her teeth, for effect.

Nancy laughed and shushed her. "He may have stopped coming in, but it still feels like his eyes are here, watching us."

"And his ears?" Martha held onto her ears and wiggled them.

"And his penis." Betsy was only half-smiling.

Thuds and shouts were still coming from outside the window, and when Nancy looked in that direction this time and began to walk toward them, Martha glared at her. Nancy couldn't imagine why she looked so mean. They'd gone to karaoke together and sung their hearts out the night before. But there was no denying that when Nancy started saying, "What's that sound?" Martha shushed her invisibly while clearing her throat, widening her eyes, tightening her lips, and dropping a notebook.

Nancy forgot about the mysterious clangs outside when she heard the front door close and heard the words, "Mail call!" Her heart beat faster, her cheeks growing hot. She dropped her head so her bangs would frame her green eyes fetchingly, as she glanced toward the door, where the young delivery man named Julio had been quietly standing with several pieces of equipment to distribute. Oh, no, he'd heard the penis comment!

She yanked the hair tie, which got caught in her short strawberry blonde hair. She twisted it, trying to detangle, and tugged so hard she pulled out a lock, which she hid in her pocket. She thought about split ends and she thought about frizz: she turned away from him so maybe he wouldn't notice her.

She wished he'd come in a little earlier and learned that she competed in karate. Guys she met usually found that to be hot.

4

Martha offered him a candy from the plastic bowl on her desk.

"Thank you. But is it milk chocolate?" He nodded gratefully.

"Who cares? A little won't hurt you."

"No, that's OK."

"You know you want to." Martha's voice became campily sultry, which made Nancy turn around to observe the sudden shift. She'd seen Martha vamp before. She just couldn't remember when.

"Sorry, I'm a vegan," he said, running his hands through his thick, shiny black hair.

Nancy cringed. He'd never like her, considering she helped the process of making and selling poisons that killed not only insects but raccoons, pigeons, mice – and anything that ate those unfortunate creatures. How many owls had died because of D-CIDE? She did her best not to think about it so much it crippled her ability to do anything at all.

She wanted desperately to assuage her guilt over her job at a company that killed creatures. Humans were such brutes. The image entered her mind of running an animal sanctuary, while dressed like an astonishingly beautiful penitent nun, or maybe a mendicant wearing a low-cut hair shirt, more of a primitive shift, really. She'd tangle her hair and grow it out to get the wild-woman look. She'd let sticks fall in it and let them stay, like a bird's nest. She would work there with Julio watching, proud of her for eventually saving all the wild animals of the world. The animal-to-human ratio would normalize. She and Julio would kiss to swelling music. It would be grand.

She couldn't help extra blood flowing to her cheeks when she looked at him, as he handed one of the workers a package. Why couldn't extra blood go to the waist, the back, anywhere less obvious than a blush? She put her hand over her face, tentatively, then decided that looked silly and clumsily moved a strand of hair behind her ear, trying to look natural.

Though she wanted to watch Julio walk as he took a different package to the office manager across the large room, Nancy's attention was diverted to the cranking, humming sound outside. While she wouldn't have normally gone to the window and opened the blinds to identify a random sound, this time it gave her a welcome chance to leave the uncomfortable conversation. She pulled her hair in front of her and smoothed out the tangles with her fingers.

A large truck was idling beside the faded storage module in the back of the plant. The office workers liked to call the imposing gray storage unit "Old Faithful." Nancy was well used to seeing the module, the largest, thickest, and most secure containment available. Martha had joked about the EPA rules against either using or dumping the XXX poison housed inside the only type of storage container allowed by the regulations when she wrote the check for the yearly rental fee.

When, years ago, Martha had said, "When is Old Faithful going to erupt and end the known universe?" Nancy had dreamed that night about the cans inside it, which had become fragile and eaten away by the unparalleled toxicity over the decades, during which they exceeded the expiration date. They had exploded, covering her face with burns, and melting her immediately as she seeped into the heating vents; then evaporated slowly into the office as a kind of smelly afterlife.

Nancy watched workers raising the huge module to the truck. When she started to say something about it, she felt as if something were grabbing her throat from the inside and keeping her from speaking. She tried, and only stuttered strangely garbled sounds.

Martha laughed. "What's up, girl, have you started speaking in tongues?" Martha raised her hands in the air and nodded her head, her eyes closed like an earnest Pentecostal. She mumbled incomprehensible syllables that sounded goofier and goofier the longer she teased Nancy.

Nancy tried to laugh at the good show but gulped, putting her hand to her throat, and looked away. A whole world seemed to be trying to come out of her mouth and simultaneously jump down inside the abyss opening inside her to swallow it whole.

She surreptitiously pulled an archival folder from the shelves, when no one was looking, and rifled through the ledger, finding nothing showing the module scheduled for pickup. Martha would need to sign off with the rental company to get the deposit back, but she saw nothing arranged for that.

The containers of XXX that filled up the module weren't registered, being too old. The XXX had no restrictions for tracking because it was produced too long ago to have modern labels. She knew of no new laws that would allow D-CIDE to stop storing the poison that had been in their main pesticide products decades before. There would have been a big party if there had been a new rule, and her uncle would have gotten drunk and pressured his prettiest employees into kissing him, in front of everyone, if they wanted to keep their jobs.

Had perhaps a new EPA rule gone into place after he recently left his managerial position, and he hadn't sent the message to anyone? Surely not. He would have come into the office just so he could gloat. He would have joked about revenge. He had built his life around killing pests with that core ingredient until he was slapped down without any compensation from the EPA.

Nancy was glad she was related to him and thus off-limits for being treated as a sex object. Otherwise, she would have never been able to keep her job as comfortably as she did. Her uncle Geoff Buzner was the only boss she'd ever been able to work for, for any length of time. People who suddenly came to consciousness, bewildered by where they'd been for several missing hours, weren't generally the studs of steady employment.

And then, there was the little fact of the illicit pills, called Jolly Wests, that her uncle supplied her for free. Yes, there was that.

Geoff seemed to have an uncanny patience about her amnesiac fugues. And though he'd caught her in compromising circumstances, he had not reported her. Yet, she realized she was ironically on a trajectory of reporting *him* for an illegal dumping crime. She was an ingrate.

He would hate her beyond measure. She shivered and felt hot at the same time. Her jaw muscles tightened, pulling in her chin. She stretched her jaw forward, making sure Julio couldn't see her looking like a bottom-feeding ocean fish.

She thought perhaps the waste management company had made a mistake, or someone at the office had screwed up when arranging pickup of the XXX. Dumping it would endanger the lives of not only any people who went to the dump, but also animals who poked around, plants trying to grow, and groundwater. It could kill from contact with the skin. Women living near the dumps where XXX was placed decades in the past had been found with massive amounts of it in their breast milk, and their children were born with defects and diabetes. Many cases of cancer were attributed to the toxins. She knew cans would break upon impact with the rubble and whichever ones didn't break would erode immediately in the elements.

The dump should become a Superfund if it had XXX in it. She might have to be the one to alert the authorities. If she managed to stop the dumping, or at least got the location turned into a Superfund, she certainly couldn't ask her uncle Geoff for a recommendation for her to work elsewhere after D-CIDE was shut down for illegal activity.

If she did anything, would that lead to punishment and permanent unemployment? Would she find herself living on the streets begging for dollars? Would she ever be able to beg for money? Or would she just lie down and die? She'd never been able to ask people for things. Would Geoff find a way to set her up and put her behind bars instead?

Or worse. She suspected he had zero compunction about arranging a person's death. The thought made her throat close up, and she gasped for air, coughing until she drank a sip of water. She looked around, wondering who was in on the poison crime. Who could she trust? Maybe no one.

Particles had filled the air around the dump where XXX had been poured decades before, and small wild animals and birds had been found littering the ground. Animals and plants grown for food were not supposed to be sold if the poison was dumped within fifty miles. Lots of homeless people survived because they frequented the dump, picking through everything for food and things to recycle or sell. What would happen to them? They didn't have to eat food the XXX had fallen onto. XXX could kill a person if it got on the skin and was left there for a couple of hours. Three operators working for D-CIDE had died in the past because of that.

Even worse, XXX was also carefully regulated because it was the ultimate murder weapon. It was untraceable in the body even when tested with the most advanced methods. It worked immediately and only a drop, which had no taste, stain, or smell, could kill a large man, with no recognizable symptoms. The regulations had gotten deranged through endless, expensive litigation. Murderers could go on killing sprees if they got their hands on it.

She started to ask about the waste truck picking up the poison, but her throat wouldn't let her. Why? She couldn't imagine. What the hell? Martha gave her a steady stare that seemed to penetrate her deepest being. Martha's steel-blue eyes took over the world.

Nancy gagged and covered her mouth. Something terrible was happening right at that moment and she wanted to know what it was. She didn't want to stand by hopelessly and pretend she was a good person. She didn't want to deny part of herself any more than she already did. She'd used up her quota of human denial of culpability. She had to fix the awful situation somehow. *I need redemption for my whole life. If it can be called "whole."*

The moment of silence in their conversation stretched like taffy.

She looked down at the hard floor, gauging the distance: she held her breath, grasped her head and faked fainting, doing her best not to hurt herself. She landed in a position she hoped looked attractive to Julio, who had accepted a cup of coffee from Martha and was leaning on her desk, drinking it. Nancy's neck was stretched to look long like a swan's.

"Maybe she doesn't like penises?" quipped Betsy.

So much had happened since the last sentence in their conversation, Nancy was jolted back to the present by the remark, but she had to keep the surprise from showing on her face. Nancy's co-workers gathered around her and one started to place a call to an ambulance. She roused herself. "Sorry, sorry. I'm OK. I just. Do you mind if I leave early?"

Betsy cautioned, "Sure. Just don't drive, obviously. You're pale. Who will come pick you up?"

"I'll ring a friend." She pretended to call someone, and then said, "I'll go out and get some fresh air while I wait."

As she was preparing to get in her car, Julio ran out with a bottle of water. Nancy hid her distaste for petroleum-based plastics and thanked him, moved by his concern. She sat down on the curb to drink as she watched him run back in lithely. The skin on his forearms gleamed in the sun rays that were coming through the heavy gathering rain clouds. The polarized light set him off beautifully. He turned to look back at her when he reached the door, and she marveled at how his jaw could at once seem so strong and masculine yet artistic and delicate. He was a wonder.

As he entered the building, she went to her car, which was nicely hidden, behind the others in the parking lot. She drove off quietly, until she was out of their noticeable hearing range. Then, she pushed the accelerator to the floor, which threw her head back against the headrest and zoomed off after the truck, steering around a car ahead of her in the darkness. She waited to turn on her headlights until she had to when a car swerved a little into her lane.

The adventure had begun. She kind of liked it. She'd always liked reading about girl detectives.

She followed the truck, weaving in and out of traffic and cutting corners too closely, honking her horn at anyone in her way. She managed to keep the vehicle in sight, most of the time, and trusted her intuition when she didn't. Whenever she pulled around a semi truck, there was the waste truck, in the distance. She was closing in on it, gradually. She fumbled for a cigarette, mad at herself for wasting the split second by doing so, but she had to have her fix. Damn tobacco industry. How had they gotten her hooked? Once she inhaled, she was more focused and calm as she zoomed around the cars, one after another, her body leaning to the left and the right amidst honking all around.

She'd been to the dump once, long ago. She searched her memory as she drove, trying to picture the location at the same time as avoiding killing people on the road. Then, it hit her. She knew exactly where to find it. She laughed out loud: "I got you, motherfucker!" There was no way the truck could dump its load before she got there, even if she lost track of it on the way!

Then, a watermelon truck going painfully slow ahead of her spilled some of its contents. She dodged the melons, avoiding running into any other cars by using the quick reflexes and excellent coordination she'd developed through karate. She even surprised herself by her master driving skills. She was born for the chase! The road was blocked by the rolling fruit and cars turning sideways and stopping. She slowed to an excruciating pace. *Gah!*

She gasped when she spotted an alternate route to bypass the jam. Perfect. Well, almost. The off-road was quaint. She had no time for quaint. It was sloshy from recent rain, and she nearly bogged down, spinning her wheels, until they became unstuck, throwing gritty water over her car. She looked around wildly for other routes. She got back onto the main road as fast as she could, wondering if she could be attracting the attention of traffic police. She no longer saw the waste truck and took every chance she could to zoom down the highway, doing her best to catch up. After all that, maybe it *was* possible he could complete the dump before she made it there.

By the time she neared the dump, she saw the truck ahead on the road. "Ha *ha*!" she cried. But, as she prepared to follow it into the dump, it continued down the road, rather than turning off. She was bewildered. She slammed her hand against the steering wheel.

Where was it *going*? Did the driver know she was following? Was he trying to throw her off the track?

She put more distance between them and glanced off at the dark, stormy landscape. Huge drops of water hit the windshield. The waste truck turned down a side street, and she slowed, anxious it was getting too far ahead for her to know where it was going. She hoped another truck would turn onto the street too, so she could hide behind it and not be too obviously following the waste truck if the driver looked in his rear-view mirror. That was not looking likely to happen, so she took a big chance. A death-defying, prison-defying chance.

She pulled up next to a random red truck, as if she were passing it, and then angled straight at it. The only place that driver could go to get away from her without a fatal accident on the regular road was down the side road. She followed directly behind it so she would be invisible to the waste truck driver ahead. She congratulated herself with a loud whoop. The red truck driver was shouting and pushing on the brakes but never went so far as to slam them and cause a mash-up. She sure didn't want to see that happen! What an irony that would be.

She took off her business suit jacket as she tailgated him, weaving a little to the left and right as she steered with one hand, nearly sliding off into a ditch and turning over her car. She unbuttoned her crisp white shirt and pulled her breasts out of her black lace bra.

She had to make him like her so he wouldn't report her. Desperate measures were required. She revved up and veered slightly off the road into a dead patch of grass to stir up enough thick mud to cover her license plate.

She caught his eye as she drove up next to the little red truck. She was ready to pass and take her chances. The driver of the red truck was leaning out the window, maroon-faced, yelling at her that he was going to put her in jail. He aimed his cell phone at her. She'd better leave him with a photo to drool over privately rather than send to the police. She gave him a seductive look, amplified by lifting her chest. The nipples on her milky breasts pointed in his direction. He smiled back and waved. Her ploy to pacify him had worked wonders.

The waste truck slowed down when she pulled past the other vehicle and turned off into a drive. She had to wonder if the driver had seen her suddenly showing up behind him. By the time she reached the drive, the truck was driving out again. It turned back the way it had come down the muddy little road. She made a U-turn and followed. There was no hiding what she was doing anymore.

They made it back to the highway and she kept behind him until a semi nudged in front of her and she couldn't see the waste truck anymore. She had to slow down, because rain was starting to pour, making the road slick. She didn't want to hydroplane and run into any of the flammable trucks on the road. As the rain came down harder, she had trouble seeing, and her windows became fogged.

By the time she got around the semi, the waste truck was gone. Her intuition said he had taken a ramp. She took the next one and doubled back the way she had come, in the direction of the dump. She had no idea if the waste truck really had retraced its path, but if that's where the driver originally intended it to go, she'd find it.

She would never really do it, as she had some control over her consumerism, at least when it came to toxic technology, but she almost wished she had given in and gotten a cell phone in case of an emergency: she then could take photos or even better, a video of the dumping. She would be able to call the authorities and send them the evidence. If officers showed up before too much of the chemical was leaked, at least some of the damage would be prevented, and justice could occur. But no. She had her limits as to how ready she was for brain tumors. She only used a landline.

Once she got there, she searched it thoroughly, looking for the truck. How awful, looking at the results of humanity's existence on this earth. She couldn't just turn away and pretend her refuse disappeared. She had to admit the truth of how her existence polluted the planet. Plastic containers of nasty chemicals. Why XXX would be so much more dangerous that they would be illegal to dispose of she didn't really understand. How much worse could it be? But, apparently, the EPA considered it to be so for a reason. She wanted so badly to go back home and watch a movie, practice piano, anything but face what people were dumping out of sight, out of mind.

She looked everywhere at the dump. In the dirt, in the smell, among the homeless people digging, in the sadness of humanity's destruction of the planet.

The truck was nowhere to be found.

CHAPTER TWO
Ring Ring

Nancy didn't turn on the light when walking into her apartment after the harrowing chase. She was eager to get at the laptop. Things would soon make sense. Her jitters made her spill the coffee she'd picked up at a drive-through on the way. It splashed onto her oak desk in her bedroom. She cleaned up the mess before it ruined the finish and told herself that it was a good thing, as she shouldn't be drinking it so late. But, she knew she was only kidding herself about being able to sleep after what had happened at D-CIDE. She lit a cigarette as soon as she finished her last one, and popped her pill. The Jolly Wests were running out fast.

If she turned in her uncle, how would she get more? Her hand started shaking, just thinking about cold turkey. Would she need to buy drugs from gangs? Use up all her money, at ten dollars a pill? Steal to support her habit? Or, somehow convince multiple doctors she had the rare condition that required having a couple of those pills on hand? She'd have to tell the doctors she was taking those controversial, experimental drugs only in emergencies, and then, actually pay for an ambulance, from time to time, and a hospital stay. But could she mimic the symptoms convincingly? How good was she at impersonation, really?

16

No, she wanted to be honest. She wanted to stop running from her addiction to denial. She could then turn in her uncle for a waste management crime without worrying about her fix. She liked the effect, though. Floaty, just dizzy enough to make everything a little more of a funny challenge. The pills made her confident enough to believe one day Julio might date her. Even one date would be enough to make her happy.

Stopping taking the pills would mean more of those disturbing shadowy hints of visions coming to her like they sometimes had when she'd tried to go off the drugs. The only method she'd discovered to forget the faux-memories was taking the Jollys every evening. So she'd forgotten what they were. Kids took a few pills at a time at Derealization Parties.

She'd nearly wrecked getting home because she was so curious to find out what was going on with D-CIDE. She put keywords into the search engine and clicked around from page to page. Something online *had* to explain why her uncle would let the chemicals be taken away from the company he owned and why the waste truck would carry the huge module as well as the cans. Who *did* that? And, why did the waste truck driver go to such lengths to throw her off his track? It didn't make sense. She liked it when things made sense. She *needed* them to.

And, besides, she enjoyed the feeling of being a budding detective solving the puzzle. This was going to be even better than when she'd gotten her black belt, and like she was in charge of anything that happened in her life. She quietly affirmed, "I'm doing it. I'm going after them." The sound reverberated through her room, and it seemed nothing would ever sound quite the same in her apartment again.

She ate two apples that were sitting beside her on an old pewter plate, one red and the other green. She barely took the time to thank them first, before biting into them. She picked up the bottle of cheap red wine on her desk and tried to open it without taking her eyes off the computer screen. She couldn't get the top to twist off. She hit all around the lid with her nail file, harder and harder. She grunted, picturing breaking the bottle against the side of the table and letting the wine spill down and stain. Drinking from jagged edges, little pieces of glass sliding into her throat. She slammed the lid against the corner, taking her chances.

That loosened it enough that when she lifted up her shirt and gripped the bottle with the fabric in her hand, she was able to open it. She swigged, as she speed-read about the waste management rules for XXX.

She started to scratch her back, but it wasn't an itch. What dumping those chemicals would do to the aquifer, animals, anything coming in touch with it was sending scratchy chills up her spine. It was bad enough that D-CIDE chemicals killed innocent ants. And, for some reason, the dumping seemed worse to her than seemed rational. Why the hell did it matter to her so much? That was the real question. Why was she shaking?

It wasn't really so much the toxicity in the dump that bothered her. It wasn't even the potential of it being shipped to a third-world country with more lax environmental rules because they couldn't afford to turn down dumping it. It was maybe the sleazy, clandestine nature of what was apparently going on around her, which she'd been unaware of, headed by her only living immediate relative. She was involved by proxy in a criminal act, by working for D-CIDE.

I'm a fighter, she told herself, *and I'll fucking fight.*

What that required was action: a small candy bar she could just reach without taking her eyes off the website. She had hidden it from her impulsiveness, beneath the single pillow on her bed.

Her slender body only showed such dietary indiscretions, just barely, in the extra roundness of her bottom. Her karate training kept her sinews stretched and her bones alive. As she read, under her desk she lifted up her legs, putting them down, for exercise. She liked to be a bitch worth giving a wide berth to on the street, in spite of weighing only a hundred and ten pounds.

She decided not to think about a street fight too long. She excused the dubious bruises and cuts that arose from her dissociative fugues: she couldn't take responsibility if she was too much of a trouble-maker when she was sleepwalking, could she? But, if the police found out about whatever scrapes she got into, they might think differently.

Taking an enthusiastic draw on her cigarette, she winked at herself in the mirror propped behind the desk, with an exaggerated expression like a drag queen. The light from the laptop made her look as if she were wearing cheap blue eye shadow all the way to her brows the way Martha did. Her beautiful hair was frizzled from the rain and her mascara was running.

She read in the dark about the EPA rule, made before she was born, banning the XXX chemical from being produced, sold, or dumped. That, she already knew. There had to be more.

D-CIDE executives had been disgruntled about paying for storage forever: perhaps it wasn't fair to expect them to pay for storing it indefinitely. Her feeling was that it wasn't *unfair*, either, considering they'd manufactured and spread products such as chlordane. Operators had put chlordane under and on people's floors giving countless people cancer, diabetes, and other horrible diseases. Those houses were condemned.

She despised working part-time at D-CIDE in spite of the playful camaraderie. She had nightmares about children

19

the chlordane affected, outgassed from the foundations of houses for decades. She, herself, had contracted a mild case of Acquired Porphyria from the chlordane. She was poisoned by it, giving her that illness, when she was a baby. Her parents had been snookered by D-CIDE's service branch. The operator poured termite protection down into heating vents she clambered over. He'd poured it around the edges of all the floors, where her tender hands quickly went.

When her uncle had come to the house, soon after the ban on chlordane went into effect, he had cursed about it in a way she found profoundly frightening. She had gone into her room to hide, but he had followed her in. The thick skin on his square face was red, and his pores were huge. She remembered nothing but the beautifully whimsical story she had written that night about flying out of the window of the black and white room into a colorful land in the sky.

She'd thought she was going to be a writer and illustrator of children's books and become famous. Instead, she'd taken the job at D-CIDE when she was old enough, though it meant she saw her unpleasant uncle a few times a week. She was relieved when he recently gave up managerial functions; she saw him much less often at work. Her skin even cleared up and she could breathe more fully.

She'd only let herself ponder whether he was evil once before, when her parents died suddenly and simultaneously of mysterious causes. Geoff had eagerly taken over as her legal guardian. She was grateful for his support with poison profits and gambling money. She didn't dare mention to anyone that she wondered if he had killed her parents. She shoved the idea under the bed. But in half-remembered dreams, she was chased by monsters that came out from under her bed. Her scariest dream involved her father's skull wailing that her uncle had killed him.

She put out her half-smoked cigarette in the present from Martha - a gaudy ceramic ashtray shaped like a pink upturned hand with red fingernails - and she slapped her mouth with her own unpainted fingers. She *would* quit smoking. She would. Get rid of chemicals. She'd been doing better, until the event earlier that day. That evening she was shoving chemicals down her throat to deal with how the company was shoving chemicals into the ground.

She searched the EPA's site, looking for new rules making the removal of the chemical legal, changes in the Resource Conservation and Recovery Act. When the radio music got to a swelling song that brought wine tears to her eyes, she asserted it was up to her to see what could be done about XXX, even sacrificing her future. Sure, she might end up homeless. Geoff could easily kill her in revenge, with a drop of XXX, and no one would know. She lifted up her wine bottle to toast the drama inherent in the universe. She would prevail instead of looking away, even if it took her very existence.

The birds outside her window burst into spectacular song, in defiance of the storm. Maybe she *could* just ignore the XXX thing. She could keep her job and live there and hear the songbirds in the trees outside her window. She could make her own song, make music. That was enough. She was almost ready for recitals. Her piano teacher had told her, a year before. He'd said she just had to push herself into all her corners, until she was able to play with enough depth. She could continue to go to work a few days a week and pretend nothing was wrong with the company and sleep and practice the other days of the week.

She called her elderly piano teacher and set up an appointment for him to come to her apartment. It had been a long time. She was glad for the joy in his voice.

She watched the birds hopping about on the ground. She thought about what would happen to the birds if they landed in the dump where the XXX had fallen.

No.

She would take that motherfucker Geoff *downtown*.

She looked up the phone number to report a hazardous waste crime and recommend a location be addressed as a Superfund. She was tired of no one looking into whether Geoff had committed a crime.

The woman who answered the phone was kind about taking the message. Then, she said, "One moment please. I'll transfer you to the director, Geoff Buzner."

What!

Nancy's hand grasped the old-fashioned phone more tightly. *That* was the job her uncle had taken when he gave up his managerial position with D-CIDE. No doubt that was *why* he changed jobs.

With conflict of interest, while maintaining ownership of D-CIDE, he'd left running the business to others so he could become the person responsible for deciding how those chemicals were dumped! He'd kept D-CIDE from paying premium prices for secure toxin storage, month after month, decade after decade. She was revolted. Stunned, mouth open, she forgot to put the receiver down.

"Hello, Geoff Buzner here. What can I do for you? I see according to my notes you saw someone dumping XXX? How do you *know* what it was, miss…What was your name?"

She covered her mouth when she gasped.

She changed her voice to make it sound gravelly and old. "Anne Glastonbury." She hung up immediately, the phone wet in her palm.

What if he knew what number she was calling from or could find out? He was familiar with it, calling her more than she liked, over the years. She felt clammy, and got up and

22

paced, flipping her shirt to bring air underneath it to evaporate the moisture. Her uncle was capable of any degree of revenge.

So there was the question. How do you a report a crime when the person to report the crime to *is* the criminal?

The phone rang.

Her heart nearly jumped out of her ribcage. Her startle response made her bite her tongue.

Ring.

Ring.

What if he'd taken the time to get the secretary to check the phone number? What if he'd guessed?

Ring. Stop, stop! Stop!

She ground out her cigarette in the pink palm, and coughed, drank some water, staring into the clarity. She girded her loins and threw her cigarette pack toward the trash with a jerky nod. She could tell by the sound that the pack didn't make it into the trash bin, but she left it on the floor. Fuck it.

Knowing ECHELON recorded people's calls and later other programs recorded internet searches, emails, everything, she wondered why so many people were surprised when the NSA revelations came out. That was nothing new. She felt uncomfortable as she suspected she'd triggered their attention by keywords. The agencies could be logging her keystrokes, analyzing what she was doing as she hesitated, overwrote, and deleted files. She'd felt so free when growing up when she'd let go of the notion of a God listening to her every thought. But, at least God wouldn't knock her off for trying to report damning information. Or would He?

What if there was a God, and He took a job as a paid troll? She laughed nervously, imagining Him ruining people's reputations if they didn't go along with the party line and shut up. God writing insults about people on social media if they stopped putting enough money in the collection basket. She wondered what kind of currency God would crave. Maybe He liked drugs. She could turn Him on to her pills. They weren't very exciting, but they weren't bad, either.

Who *was* her uncle Geoff really? She wanted to know more. What would drive a man to do something so destructive as to dump XXX? If he could do that, could he also have killed her parents? Of course he'd kept using the pesticide as long as he could, lobbying for it not to be banned in the early 80's. He'd obviously cared about money more than people's lives. And the plant had dumped their waste back then in the adjacent lot they left vacant and overgrown with weeds, in the midst of that low-income neighborhood. He'd never gone to prison for the deaths of local people. If he had, she would have been turned over to a different guardian, and she wouldn't have a job - or the pills.

Children had played in the tall grasses by the chemical plant, chasing each other, tackling and tickling, and then later, dying. Nothing had ever been done about it, because that kind of thing was a matter of course back then, before regulations were instated. People let it go in that neighborhood, though they wouldn't have if it had been upscale. Nancy wondered if there would have been a stink made if the children had been Caucasian.

Geoff had hated that transition to public awareness and the authors like Rachel Carson who wrote books about environmental destruction, making it a buzzword, turning people against companies like D-CIDE and Velsicol. How anyone could have thought using chemical pesticides could be safe Nancy never knew.

Ring!

She didn't move. She barely breathed. She grasped the bottom of her seat with the tips of her fingers. Somehow her body thought that if she didn't move he couldn't see her.

Once the phone stopped ringing, she called *69. She wasn't familiar with the number. If he was calling from a landline in his office, it wouldn't be the same one she'd called earlier. Maybe he had a new dedicated cell phone for that job. She looked it up, but it was unlisted.

She threw caution to the wind and looked up Geoff Buzner online again to see what she could learn about him, feeling stupid when she made typing errors. She imagined people laughing at her if her keystrokes were being logged. She found almost nothing, just the legal details about the business, such as it being registered to him, and the address.

She delved deeper, trying every keyword she could think of. She bought access to his records.

She used her decent coding skills to find her way into a website no longer online. She discovered his name mentioned without any attribution in the small print among many other names in a page buried in a large website for an international evangelical Pentecostal ministry associated with Reverend Terry Crank. She wondered if that would give any insight into her uncle's behavior and where the poison might have gone. It was a long shot. Geoff was apparently an integral part of the ministry.

Geoff had never mentioned that, though he'd had plenty of time: she'd started living with him when she was orphaned at sixteen, and stayed with him until she graduated high school. The name of the ministry sounded familiar, in a way she didn't understand. Familiar down in her bones, in her tendons, in her memories she didn't even have, her dreams she was yet to dream.

She sobbed, her gut telling her something beyond words, beyond memory, something visceral and deep. She read on through the tears, the blood escaping from the peripheries to the core of her body, away from such an awful world. She grew cold, her lips dry. When she stood up to get water, she stumbled. She knocked her laptop off the desk.

She looked away from the mirror when she walked past it to retrieve the computer. She always expected to see herself looking even younger than her already deceptively young appearance. It was almost as if she never aged; but she had. Her dark secret to remaining cute and strangely perfect: being dependent on her uncle to take care of her. People always talked about feeling as if they were younger than their years. Apparently, it was nothing unusual, she told herself. Lots of people were dependent on something.

It hit her. No wonder D-CIDE had the reverse of the ministry's triangle logo at the bottom of its website, next to the regular one. Her uncle was an important part of both organizations. There was some serious partnership going on. She'd always thought the symbol on the site was just decoration. But the ministry's logo was a highly stylized upward pointing triangle of the exact same style, size, shape, and dark blue color as D-CIDE's, just vertically reversed. Seeing the triangles created an acrid tingle along her skin. She felt as if she were burning. Maybe that had something to do with the prank when the saleswoman tried to make her believe there were upward and downward pointing triangles on her calendar? What was that about?

Something about the combination of two triangles made her reach for her wine and swig it, trying not to cry. She would be a tough bitch. She would be a trouble-maker. Not a wuss.

And, no wonder Geoff required Martha's persona as a devout Christian, telling people on the phone, "Oh bless you, darling. God loves you. You'll be so glad you bought this from us." Her supposed piety reflected well on Geoff, in his religious community.

Martha tended to tell complaining customers that God would forgive them for insulting D-CIDE. Martha didn't bother pretending to love Jesus all the time around the people in the office like she did with the customers. Keeping up that holy ruse would surely maim someone that crass. Nancy would require a note delivered from God Himself to believe her uncle loved and feared Him. And Nancy didn't even *believe* in God.

Nancy's pulse raced. She wanted to have some evidence for the police about where the waste management people had taken the illegal stuff. If she was going to get her uncle arrested, she wanted it to be a solid enough case to lock him up immediately, with no way he could get out of it and come after her.

She was afraid he would lie about abusing the conflict of interest of his regulatory position and come get her. Of course, maybe his associates could track her down at any moment. She hadn't found evidence the rule had been legally changed. It could have been a good ol' boys agreement. But *maybe* the rules had been changed, and if she reported him, he would punish her. She could barely stand not knowing. Yet, who could she ask? Geoff?

He could convince people she was just nuts, by showing evidence of her sleepwalking or whatever the hell it was that caused her to have so many anomalies and so much missing time. He could get her institutionalized for life.

The clock was ticking away the moments, as XXX seeped from the old containers that would have cracked when dumped onto all the rubble. The poison had to have drastically weakened the containers after decades. The people in the office had joked about it enough she'd pictured it, even dreamed of it. She got lost in how many people, plants, and animals her uncle was murdering as the broken cans leaked at the dump.

In the past, D-CIDE had bought massive quantities of chlordane from Velsicol. Until 1978, Velsicol had sent their waste to a dump in Tennessee. Contamination was discovered in wells in the area, and they had to stop. She studied that history and everything else she could find on the topic, her eyes burning, her eyelids tiring. She wanted to rest, but her quest didn't allow her to.

She steeled herself against disappointment. Superfund status usually took years to obtain, as the process ate up money, day after day. Then, the officials traditionally took the poisoned material and dumped it in *other* sites instead. The alternate sites were often even less prepared to contain the poisons than the original site had been. What was a hero to do?

Sudden pain gripped her throat. She didn't understand. It felt like a fire burning her.

Swallowing was difficult. The center of the bottom of her neck felt hot and inflamed.

She felt incredibly stupid, wondering if some Agent of the Nevermind had triangulated directed energy beams above her clavicle as a warning. Her karate buddy, Alyssa, had recently told her about how such things were possible and Nancy had only laughed. Alyssa had turned away with a hurt look. Nancy knew Alyssa was smart, so she'd made herself stop laughing.

She wouldn't tell *anyone* she thought about a direct energy beam attack. *Ever.* Not even Alyssa. She looked it up online to read about EMF-targeted individuals. The creepiest part was thinking someone could have been watching her search. One more paranoid nut gone wild.

Was it gluten making her think that way and giving her a rash as it went down her throat? She tried to remember if she'd had any of that forbidden substance within the last few days. She would hate for someone to think she was a conspiracy theorist. A wacko. A joke.

In the mirror. . . A perfectly round bright red thick welt stood out on the center of her neck. Hideous. She clutched it as if she could cover it up to make it go away, nearly strangling herself. When she pulled her hand away, a choker necklace of light pink from her squeeze, with the perfect red circle, decorated the middle.

She'd never had an allergic reaction like that. There was that shot of vodka the day before. . . She looked it up online. Her eyes felt blurry. Did she need to go to the doctor? But search engine results had always told her more useful information than her doctors had. *Hmm. That's potatoes, right? But no. It's grains. Sneaky. It caused some people to have gluten reactions.*

Her responses to that protein sometimes made her get a little carried away with things. Odd things. Maybe that happened with vodka. She'd never noticed that pattern. *Certainly* never a precise round welt with perfect edges and proportions in the soft spot where the clavicle, breastbone, and neck come together.

She wanted to drink *more* vodka to calm down but instead decided to give her body a break. Even commercial wine with all the pesticides in it had lost its appeal. The organic kind was awfully expensive. Chemicals were sickening; it was time to rebel. Glad she was passed over for a promotion to manager at work, she would not have to grow up to be a Chemical Queen.

Time to give it a break. With the suspicious phone calls she didn't want to risk it in case her searches online were being heavily monitored. Maybe they were a warning against reporting the waste management crime. She was fidgety, anyway.

She got up and played her piano on the other side of the room, trying to keep her eyes from straying to her desk. Instead, she made herself focus on the triptych on her wall: three beautiful images of classical pianists playing, with richly colored sumptuous costume, and rapturous audiences.

In the middle of a song, her concentration stopped. She tried to resist going straight back to the laptop and drawing more attention to her searches online and instead made herself a salad. Why did she have such a sugar craving, and why had she gained weight? She hardly ate anything but diet food — other than the lapses. She practiced karate for a few minutes after she ate, putting all her power into the kicks.

When she washed the dishes, she wiped the counter with her sponge and nicked an ant. When she lifted the sponge quickly and peered into it, she saw the insect struggling, lifting all its legs but one, as it tried to pull itself across the wet surface. She couldn't tell if it was stuck or broken, if that was temporary or permanent. She felt terrible for doing that to it. She reached down with her fork prong to try to lift its leg. She looked more closely, trying to determine if she had helped or hurt. She couldn't tell, but if she hadn't helped, the ant must have felt horrified by her gigantic green eyes coming toward it.

Even worse, she saw another one come along and begin to drag it.

Beside it another ant walked, carrying a dead one out of the sink.

She hated herself.

There was no fucking reason humans should ruin the lives of everything around them and fucking continue to exist. She couldn't think about it too hard. She wanted to just die. She thought about the pesticides. XXX wasn't any worse than the rest, really. That was the thing. They were all terrible. She just couldn't stand to think about it long enough to really get that. She wanted to escape, to escape, damn it, and be like a little girl. Read a stupid illustrated book about zombies and vampires.

Yet, she thought about all the plastic bottles she'd thrown away floating in the ocean killing birds. She thought about the job she'd had before, working in a water bottling plant. She thought about clearcut forests. The wood floor she was walking on. She just wanted redemption from that. That's what her XXX trail was about. Putting the blame for her selfish humanity on someone else. And making him suffer.

She cleaned up the house, scrubbing the dirt hard out of the floor, crying for the tree, talking to it, apologizing to it. She floated into the wood grain and she became nature itself, playful, bright, sunny, photosynthesizing.... She breathed.

Finally, she felt she'd earned more computer time. She checked the narcolepsy forum, putting in her username, INoSeeMe***. That wouldn't look suspicious. She checked the keyword "sleepwalking," as usual, and sighed. Why was she so different from the others? What they described sounded little like her symptoms.

She checked her social media. That should be fine. A cute cat video from Alyssa, a recommendation from her piano group, environmental petitions. And of *course* she had one of those quirky, slightly incomprehensible sweet messages from the man named Jeff who lived in the southern part of the state. It was hard to get over his name, which was so much like her uncle's. She'd never met him, but his face looked kind and handsome. He was around her age and put up inspirational quotes, pictures of mountains and oceans, meditation videos and funny memes. And he seemed poetic and interested in her more than just for her looks. He would be a good inspiration to her for quitting chemicals. He was into all things natural, and that inspired her to push herself away again from the computer.

She crossed her room, determined to play the entire *Drei Klavierstücke* — three integrated piano pieces by the Austrian composer, Arnold Schoenberg, written in 1909, based on three-note intervallic cells. Schoenberg's projection of some of the material from the first piece into the other two pieces created a kind of dissonant, atonal cohesion that she loved. The repeating three-note motif made her feel almost complete, yet expressed the strangeness she felt at her core.

The pieces broke into the three-note motifs as if the entire world were made only out of them. The motifs stuck together as if in love with each other, clinging fiercely, becoming one in so many ways, on so many levels, they transcended any kind of structure that would hold them in, and they became wild and free. The music became more violent, full of divergent emotions that shocked each other with their nearness. The music was imbalanced, never matured or completed, just continued, dreamlike, until it was done. It was her favorite music. It was her.

Then, after the flourish at the finale, she tried playing around with a song she'd written as a child, which haunted her. She never felt she got it right at all. It seemed so thin and simple, as if something was missing: most of it, in fact. When she first wrote it, the song was full and transformative. It was important, and she didn't know why, but she felt as if her continued existence rested on remembering the rest of the song.

She kept twiddling, tweaking it, distractedly playing the melody with one hand. But the rest wouldn't come to her. It was the kind of tune one might hear in some kind of distant dream. She mused on a fantasy of stepping over a colorful puddle of oil swirling with water, reflecting a sunset one walked into and never returned from...

32

She opened her eyes and jumped when the phone rang. How far would he go to eliminate the threat?

Ring. Where was he calling from? At home, his new office, or *outside her house*?

Ring. It could be anyone.

Ring. She practiced karate again, punching the sound of the phone, punching the warning, kicking the possibility of losing her job, her freedom, her life.

CHAPTER THREE
Revelations

Nancy met her practice partner, Alyssa, at her house the next day for their usual early breakfast to practice. They planned to compete in a tournament that evening. The two of them prepared a fruit plate together, marveling over the lush pink insides of the plump figs and the orange and yellow of the peaches contrasting with the lush gray of the granite counter and giant maroon bowl.

Alyssa massaged Nancy's shoulders and said, "I tried calling you, even pretty late last night. Guess you were doing your narcolepsy thing? Or were you out with a guy? Something you haven't told me, hmm?" Alyssa tossed her long, straight, black hair over her shoulder and twirled her straight-cut bangs while she smirked.

Maybe Geoff didn't figure out it was me, after all. Maybe all those calls were from random people, like Alyssa.

But who was calling the time she checked? That one wasn't Alyssa's number. She put it down to chance timing. *Things happen. Some salesman, maybe.*

Alyssa said, "Oh well, pray tell," in a nasal voice as she mimicked a cartoon character they liked, and Nancy followed suit. They acted out a ridiculous scene they'd watched that week.

"Your prayers are answered." Alyssa pretended to be a bee and did an overly enthusiastic bee-waggle-dance.

As they stretched in the living room, Nancy said, "Get this. My uncle is now making the rules for waste management in the entire state. He might even have made a rule allowing his company to dump nasty chemicals. I can't tell yet. Can you believe it? Disgusting."

"Well, you know waste management companies are famous for being as corrupt as it gets, right?"

"That's weird," said Nancy. "Seems sort of out of left field."

"A lot of the legit ones are run out of business by the mob. The gangs undercut their prices because they haul and dump stuff that's not allowed to be. They hide the toxic stuff there so they aren't taxed as much for it. They change the paperwork and mess with the scales. They launder money from their other crimes like gambling and prostitution. People put themselves on the payroll and never do anything." Her low, husky voice trailed off.

Was Geoff a *mobster*? Nancy had never thought of that. That would explain a lot. Sort of. "Was that on the news or something?"

"No, well, I guess 'famous' is the wrong word. For people who get their facts that way, I doubt it's a popular topic. But you know how the media is. They have to pander to the corporations that fund them. And the CIA in the past, and the Nevermind of course, now."

Nancy laughed. "Oh come on. What does the CIA have to do with the news?"

"Seriously? Don't you know about Operation Mockingbird? Nancy, Nancy, Nancy. I thought you had a clue, girl. Come on."

That stung. She hated feeling stupid around her educated friend. "No. That's a pretty funny name though."

Nancy hadn't talked about such topics with Alyssa for a long time. Alyssa was well-educated, though she downplayed it around her. Alyssa had been the first one to clue Nancy in about surveillance by ECHELON before surveillance became the mainstream cool thing to get riled up about, sending her a documentary about it by the secretive independent YouTube journalist Elias Brandon. Alyssa had told her the history about how the Agency of the Nevermind had come about in the 80's in the time of the Human Growth Hormone-created giants. She'd told her about the CIA's MKULTRA project and how some of its tactics had been continued by the Nevermind, using hypnosis, drugs, theatrics, popular entertainment and the occult.

Nancy was so scared afterward she had tried not to think about it anymore. But this angle with the newscasters was uncharted territory. She couldn't figure out herself why she hadn't suspected all along. How blind was she?

"It all came out in the '70s, with the Church Report. Check it out sometime, chica. At the end of the Cold War, the CIA's Office of Special Projects started the rule: the news had to be run by them first so they didn't say the wrong thing. Plus the CFR has to check everything over."

"Why?"

"So they tell the proper lies for social engineering the society. You know, make them love or hate the right foreign leaders and whatever the hot trend is at the moment. Hell, most mainstream newscasters and journalists *are* agents. They're mostly in the Nevermind, of course now that it's stepped up to manage disinformation magick. And of course they're working with the OSI."

"Holy moly." Nancy covered her mouth.

"Not that it necessarily has anything to do with waste management, but who knows? If they never made more of a stink on the news about all the horrendous things that the companies did year after year, they must be protecting them for some reason. That's why I like getting the scoop from Elias Brandon instead. He tells it like it is."

"Yeah, yeah, Brandon. Do you know how much you talk about your idol? Is he ever wrong?" She felt jealous of the man Alyssa quoted so often, who knew everything Nancy didn't. Who would her best friend Alyssa choose if there was only one other person surviving in the world? Elias Brandon. She knew it. And they'd have kids and start the whole stupid world again. He never showed his face on the videos. But his low, booming voice was sexy enough Nancy just knew Alyssa had to like him better than she liked her. Even if he did have gigantism like the rumors suggested.

"Look, Nancy. I know he supposedly lives around here, but it's not like I'm going to hang out with him. Are you?"

'No, you're going to waste your time with stupid ol' me. It's not my fault Geoff took me out of school once I turned sixteen and made me earn my keep at D-CIDE." Nancy tried to make the bubbling feeling in her chest go away. She was glad she got to kick toward Alyssa. Nancy looked at the clock. She cared more about Crank than about the tournament. Asking Geoff directly about the poison would have been prohibitively improper. She needed clues.

Alyssa grabbed Nancy's hands roughly. "Let's get started practicing... So, you do know about garbage mobsters, right?"

Nancy giggled. "Now *you've* got to be kidding." Then she frowned. "Are you pulling my leg? I'm not that dumb, Alyssa!"

"No, seriously. Waste management firms really tend to be crooked business practices. You never heard about the death threats? The disappearances?" Alyssa then began the practice, punching and kicking, sliding and ducking, drawing Nancy into the fight.

Nancy's aim was off, her kicks hesitant, her eyes wandering. She barely registered the familiar shelves filled with thick books and documentary DVDs. Her eyes skimmed over Alyssa's history Ph.D. certificate framed on the salmon-colored wall. She broke their rules about talking while practicing karate. "So, if you follow the secret news, then – *ouch*!"

"What are you doing? You call that a kick? That won't win you any points at the tourney." Alyssa dodged her and grabbed her foot, twirling her around without obeying the rules of karate, either.

"I'm sorry; I'm somewhere else," Nancy said, while catching her balance and kicking, as she spun around again and grabbed Alyssa awkwardly.

"Obviously. Well, not obviously. You don't have to go to the meet. We don't have to warm up."

"I don't want to disappoint my Sensei."

"*Haiya*! OK, then, what?" Alyssa's hair was falling into her eyes, and she blew upwards at her bangs.

"Listen. Do you know anything about Terry Crank?" That tall, slender fire and brimstone Reverend, always in a dark suit, usually sporting an accusatory grimace.

"*The* Terry Crank? Evangelist jerk? Of course."

"He's a jerk?"

Alyssa laughed and ran toward Nancy with a grin. Nancy went off bounds on the mat and backed up as the taller woman came at her with dirty tricks.

"He's awful. According to some writers I've read, his ministry was apparently involved in a massive mind control plot working together with the CIA for decades, and then he supposedly switched to the Nevermind because there's some wacky occult stuff going on. If that's what you're driving at. I wish I still had the book I read years ago that had a good chapter on him. I forget what it was called. Elias Brandon has a video that talks about him."

"Of *course* he does. Isn't it illegal to out agents? How does Brandon get away with that shit if it's true?"

"Sure, but outing them has almost never gone to court. You can't keep that stuff secret forever. Even the women who accused Crank in their memoirs about being mind-control couriers for the CIA and Nevermind never got in trouble."

"Strange little cultural pastime, arguing about who is Nevermind and who isn't." Nancy made a sibilant *psspspsps* sound, like a group of gossipers.

"And never knowing if the person you're talking to really looks like you think they do. Because the Nevermind could have hypnotized you to make you see her however they want you to."

"Sort of a puzzle they've made of our lives, here in the good old United States of Confusion."

"Not just in this country. Obviously, the Nevermind is active almost as much in England as it is here. The Tavistock will never die. But they get their hands dirty in every country that has any value. It's fun to read the clues and figure out what's going on in the world around you. Isn't it? Once you put the puzzle together, it's damn liberating to see how you've been duped in the past. And most people still have the wool pulled over their eyes. You should really just watch more Brandon." Alyssa's kick barely missed Nancy's head,

"Maybe he should watch me!" Nancy bent over and pulled down her pants, mooning her friend, who didn't laugh.

"What's wrong, kiddo? You know he's not in it for the fame, considering he's anonymous. He just actually cares about what happens in the world."

"I'm just not that into that kind of conspiracy stuff. But, seriously? A minister in the Nevermind? Kind of odd." Nancy hopped away and spun, kicking her leg high in the air. She'd been hoping he was one innocent man she could still look up to. Alyssa was a killjoy when it came to giving her the dirt on all her heroes. Crank's name was iconic, representing self-righteous goodness, the same way Mother Teresa's had once been until people looked more closely into her protection of a convicted pedophile.

"Crank's a powerful guy. Friends with world leaders, the Pope, royalty, you name it. He's tied in with that evangelical thing in the military where they're trying to convert everyone and get them to vote for the far right politicians. They say Crank and his right-hand man, who's in charge of all the chaplains in the Army, go together to all the countries and spy on their secrets so the military and Nevermind can take them down. Brandon isn't the one who came up with the info originally, but he does have a…"

Alyssa countered Nancy's move aggressively, with an awkward smack. She turned a somersault and did a "come get me" dance, bouncing from one foot to the other, fists up like a 1950s gangster.

Alyssa grabbed a napkin and dabbed her eyes, then her forehead. Her voice was pleasingly low, her bone structure classic, and her comedic expressions brilliant. "OK, kiddo, better get serious for a few minutes, anyway. I do care about how I perform today." She was younger than Nancy, but "kiddo" always seemed appropriate, anyway.

They went at it in earnest for an hour. Eventually, Nancy started to ask a question, but a foot jarring her shoulder made her rethink dividing her attention.

"You'd better get with it, girly, or you won't be in any shape for the match once I'm done with you." Alyssa threw her fastest punch, taking Nancy down. "And I'm starting vacation from the university tomorrow, going on a camping trip to our favorite mountains, eh, eh? You know how I love it at my spot. So I can't stick around and patch you up, sistah."

Nancy rolled and kicked her. Her vision clarified, and her speed returned. She was light on her feet, she bounced almost as if she were made of air. Still, she only won two of the practice tussles. Her slender, smooth cheekbone was bruised.

Nancy went to the kitchen for some ice. Even the freezer had books on top of it. This time she slowed down enough to notice what they were. Studies on U.S. history, scientific studies, epidemiology, war strategy, public relations, Edward Bernays, and the Dominionist Moral Majority influence on voters behind the scenes in the political arena.

Nancy looked around the house in a different way than she'd ever done. She'd become inquisitive and was hungry for clues to understand her world. She wanted to know about money laundering and hiding gambling debts and organized crime. Her aching face was testament to her need to notice more of what was going on around her. She wanted to be a worthwhile friend for Alyssa before she lost her because of her naiveté. She paced the living room, lifting up folders of documents sitting on a table as she tied up the mats, but her quickly darting eyes landed on nothing of any use.

Until. Her face blanched. She saw a book on the shelf that caught her eye. In fact, it was the eye of the author, Helen Marsfield, that got her attention. She felt as if someone familiar was in the room with her. As if she knew the woman. She could almost smell her. She felt sticky, tried to brush off nonexistent gunk from her clothes. She had the sense she was molting, was turning into some kind of bacterial pond.

Nancy looked through the book, hiding it from Alyssa with her body, and read: "I was in a mind control program that was working covertly through a cult called The Bee of Ra. I was brainwashed like Patty Hearst was by Donald DeFreeze." Nancy didn't know what that might mean. Alyssa had told her about Subproject 58 in which the CIA tested LSD on people as a truth serum, messing with their minds. It had upset her and made her angrier than she could explain. How could people idolize Timothy Leary and Alan Ginsberg, Ken Kesey and the rest for promoting dropping out of an active life and getting lost in illusions promoted by an Intelligence agency?

Nancy felt sorry for Helen, the author of the book, who had been victimized by CIA in the decades before that kind of work was handed over to the Agents of the Nevermind. At the same time, Helen immediately became Nancy's hero for exposing what was going on, in spite of the danger. Nancy liked that trait in anyone and it was the superpower she most wanted to gain, herself. The very thought of charging through the landscape, with the flag of freedom from illusion made Nancy's heart beat faster.

But Helen's revelation seemed like something different from the LSD project. More bizarre activities. Helen wrote that she had developed a photographic memory like the character she had obsessively identified with in an Ehroh Productions movie she'd been forced to watch repetitively, in a basement, while gagged. Freaky. Nancy flipped through more pages and came to a section of black and white photos. One picture stopped her breathing: there was Terry Crank in a publicity picture in Argentina shaking the hand of a diplomat: the diplomat had died the next day. In another, Helen was hugging a leader in Colombia who died mysteriously that night.

Nancy looked around to see if Alyssa was watching her. Her best friend was practicing kicks across the room, apparently oblivious, looking out the window.

Nancy didn't know why she didn't just ask Alyssa to borrow the book. The woman's face was too familiar; Helen seemed like one of her non-existent sisters Nancy had dreamed about flying out the window of a black and white house into a colorful world. She bent down quickly and stuck the expose' in her backpack.

She thought she heard the sound of thunder, though the day was clear. The room seemed to flash as if God were watching her theft, shining a light on her. She "saw" an image of a triangle pulse in the room. She heard Alyssa saying behind her, "Not again!"

Nancy bit her lip, blood running down it. "*Forget* the tourney!" she yelled.

She grabbed her backpack and ran out the door, crossing the threshold into a colorful world.

Her house was across town, a good run for her. She liked to be back home from practice in time for her 10:30 nap and it looked as if she was going to make it. She hyperventilated as she wondered why she had to leave suddenly.

She was already fading into dreamland as she kept up her hypnotic pace down the sidewalk when a car behind her squealed its tires loudly. She looked back, spying only the curvaceous front corner. It approached close behind her and veered off onto the sidewalk, banging and stirring up the chlorophyll smell of smashed grass.

She jumped aside, as it just barely missed her.

She turned off at the end of the block, running out of her way instead of along that street anymore. Before long, she heard the car behind her again, and she jumped into a yard with a fence, closing the gate.

A dog ran toward her across the yard, barking, its lips pulled back, teeth showing. He growled, then lunged.

She kicked him in the stomach faster than even she knew she could and flung herself over the fence onto the sidewalk.

As she ran, again the car jumped the curb and veered onto the grass behind her, slowing to her pace.

She heard the door on the passenger side, right beside and slightly behind her, open.

She ran as fast as she could go without turning around.

A strong arm wrapped around her face and covered her mouth with chloroform, while dragging her toward the car.

CHAPTER FOUR
Emily and Dog

Several blocks from Nancy's house, late that morning, Emily reached down beneath the burnished walnut pew at the Pentecostal church for the Saturday afternoon service. She twirled the frill at her hemline around one finger, watching how the rich light made little golden shadows in every accordion-fold in the off-white lace border. She was happy to be allowed to wear her short black fancy dress with the fringe of ruffles and was glad she didn't have to ever go to the plainer Sunday service at that church instead.

Sunday service was for humbler traditional people in the split congregation — the ones who engaged in regular snake-handling when the Lord anointed them to lift the writhing creatures out of their cages and used to do the other traditional practice of drinking strychnine from time to time. *Their* skirts had to cover their knees. Even the little girls. Emily didn't mind their no-makeup rule, as of course she wouldn't wear that anyway yet, but she had the distinct belief that some of the grownup ladies who attended on Sundays were too frightening without makeup. When she was even younger, their faces, with large blemishes on their noses, eyebrows missing half their hairs, and pale chapped lips, had scared her so much she'd peed her panties.

She kicked her legs up in the air and back, pounding on the pew in front of her with her feet in pink shoes with beaded flowers on them, until the angular man in the black suit turned around and glared at her. She knew how to have fun. She snagged her dress on a splinter on the curving edge of the pew. She gasped softly and looked around to see if any of the adults were mad at her for the tearing sound that sounded so loud when echoing in the giant building.

She bent her head sideways and lifted her arm up, pressing against the pew. Because she was on the end, she could hide having a sucker in her hand. She kept her arm bent by her side and the sucker hidden behind her head. She turned sideways and licked it, then turned back toward the minister. She didn't try to pay attention, but to look as if she were, her huge emerald eyes opened wide. She had made a list of her very most charming features, and her eyes were number one. She wished she could lick them. She tried, but gave up and made her tongue pointy and tried to stick it in her left nostril instead.

Her second most charming aspect was her precocious knowledge of the sixteenth-century history of Queen Elizabeth's right-hand man, John Dee, who pioneered the British Empire and provided the mathematics and instruments of navigation and research into the natural and supernatural forces aiding or abetting Britain's ability to conquer the new world. Angels were what Dee had settled on as obviously the most important force. *Who wouldn't?* she thought, and giggled.

Whenever Emily got A+ on her quizzes on Enochian language as a method to contact other dimensions and pass secrets to spies at the same time, and when she remembered all the details of the magickal system, the secret code tables and the mystery school knowledge contained inside Enochian chess, she was given suckers or cupcakes and admiring looks and pats on the head. She stored some of the suckers in her pockets so she could make it through boring old church.

She liked being petted on the head best. That made her feel like the sun was laughing. She turned back to the sucker. She was so glad she was super smart and pretty. God loved her best, she was told, and that's why she was so great. And so He talked to her through people's Enochian words that came out sometimes when they were speaking in tongues, or glossolalia, the technical term for it that she liked better, because it made her feel so smart. And He talked to her through Father. Father white with ruby, Father dead with diamond, Father of the worms.

Beside her, an elderly woman, with unadorned grayish skin, stomped in rhythm, clapping her hands beatifically. In front of her, a kind man she knew clapped his hands and looked over warmly at his wife, an upstanding woman expressing her love of life, raising her hands in the air, palms forward, lowering them, raising them again. Emily admired their innocence and purity. They had always been nice to her and everyone else.

"God bring death upon the enemy of the church!" called out an old man in a suit, with slicked back blackened hair. "Lead them unto extinction by the numbers. May Your day come upon us. Set the demons upon them!"

It was one of the special days, because Reverend Terry Crank was in town. Crank cajoled everyone to vote in the upcoming election for the Republican candidate for President of the United States. He said, "And preach the Dominion to everyone about the absolute importance of his win. We have our ambassadors for Christ in the military, evangelizing as hard as they can. Bless them. We have our men putting an end to homosexuality, feminism and abortion. Our candidate must win, and you must help him win. Tithes are not enough. No! Dig deeper, brothers and sisters. This is not the time to hold back. This is the time for theocracy. We're still paying for my plane so I can travel from country to country, preaching. And now we have the shipment of Bibles to put on it." He nodded towards his Army chaplain buddy sitting in the front pew and said, "And we have friends in high places. Like angels sitting in the clouds."

"Amen!"

Crank continued: "We must be ready to die for God's kingdom on Earth; the enemies can't be allowed to keep worshipping false gods and spreading the lies of Satan. Our God is bigger than theirs. Go forth and spread the word. And sign on to our program to travel, carrying the message to heathen countries afar."

A deacon leapt up from the second row and strode in front of them all, as Crank stepped aside for him to speak. The thick-necked deacon broke out in glossolalia, spontaneous speaking in tongues signifying the baptism of the spirit. His wide face twisted, and he stamped his foot, bending forward as he crossed back and forth in front of the members. When the cascade of syllables calmed, he continued. "The *Lord* has told me our sister congregation needs to start drinking poison at this church on Sundays again. Mark 16:18; "they will pick up snakes with their hands; and when they drink deadly poison, it will not hurt them *at all*.""

"Amen! Amen!" a few dedicated people cried out in unison. Others in the church had less convinced looks. There had always been a slight discomfort as the sister congregations did their best to avoid a rift over the difference in belief. The more intellectual, wealthier, non-snake handling congregation tended to obviously look down on the snake-handlers that met in the church on Sunday.

Martha, sans make-up, in a dowdy long skirt, sitting a few seats away on Emily's pew stood up to shout, "Amen, brother, preach it like it is! We ambassadors from the Sunday service believe the Bible in full. If you don't drink the poison and pick up the snake, you aren't going by everything the good word says. We pray for you Saturday worshippers. We believe someday you'll see the light. Our prayers are being answered, aren't they? You're coming to understand the importance of true faith."

Crank winked at Martha, and she blew him a kiss while sticking out her chest in his direction and wiggling slightly before sitting down. She tugged on her long skirt and brown loose shirt. Crank's crinkly eyes were on her every move as he smiled warmly. She played with her blonde hair and let her fingers slowly make their way down across a nipple, making it stand out.

Emily found herself fascinated by how a nipple could grow larger. She wondered if nipples were some kind of button to push that made something happen. What else could they be for? What did the button do? She tried to imagine, while also making careful note of Martha's activities. She had to keep track of the woman when she showed up from time to time in the church. Emily liked having a job like that, just like adults did.

A well-endowed woman got up from the front row and paced around with exaggerated steps next to Crank with her arms in the air, speaking glossolalia. She was overcome with the Holy Ghost, following where it led her. Crank mostly closed his eyes and held his arms out in front of him. He danced around too, his hands "happening" to land on the woman's breasts. He left them there a few seconds saying, "Bless you my child," before opening his eyes and saying, "Oh! I'd say I'm sorry but that would mean saying the Lord had led my path wrongly. The Lord is always right!"

Martha grunted loudly.

The deacon continued: "But, we *all* know they *banned* strychnine at Sunday services. If anyone is anointed by the Lord and drinks it now, the *whole* church could be in trouble. And, if someone drinks it without faith and is stricken, they'll be taken to a hospital and tested for poison in their bloodstream. Our sister congregation might have their *license* taken away for doing what they believe is necessary for them to sit by next to the Lord in Heaven. Or, maybe their kids would be taken away from them! They could be taken to *jail*. We've been fellowshipping with them and found out how awful they feel, not being able to do what the Bible commands them to do. The Lord has given me a *sign*."

Emily held Dog closer to her. The corner of the square tin box he was in pressed sharply against her skin and the thick metal coil of his body was cold against her hand. She bent her face to nuzzle his fuzzy head, closing her eyes briefly with affection.

The deacon spun and paced the other way, engaging again in glossolalia, shaking his arms flamboyantly. The velvet picture of Jesus behind him jiggled against the wall when he stomped most enthusiastically. The large congregation shuffled and moaned, shouted, and some got up and began their own obviously heartfelt glossolalia, members from the Sunday service and the regular Saturday crowd alike. Martha's voice was the most strident.

Emily brought Dog close to her face and whispered to him. She spoke in slow syllables of a language not English. When she finished the paragraphs, she sat Dog back down and kept her body still as a snake eye.

The deacon proclaimed, "The Lord has sent a man to us who can *help* us find a poison from heaven that leaves nary a *trace* in the body. No clue at all. *Ohohohohwbwbwb* it's awful stuff. It's just what our Sunday members need to *prove* their

50

allegiance to the Lord. *No* one could convict them because there would be no evidence. It's a miracle."

"Preach it!"

"And the Lord has *told* me that not only our brethren in our little town need this but *all* the Pentecostals that engage in the snake and the poison. We need to come *together* as a community and serve our fellow worshippers. The Lord has given us the *answer.* Can you hear?" He jerked his head down, leaning over, and then violently stood straight again. He ducked and stood repeatedly, and howled before moving into terraces of language. Martha stood up and opened her arms out wide.

"That was Enochian language, of course," whispered Emily to the white, floppy-eared canine head on the spring. Her favorite toy. "Are you learning much of it yet? Oh, you silly thing. You know, like when Bennu flies out the window and changes from black and white to colors, and we ride the skies. You know Bennu, the Egyptian flamingo god, right, Doggy, my dear?" She nuzzled the fur and started to lick one of the ears, but stopped when she saw Crank looking at her. "And the sky angels come singing in Enochian. Some people like to think it's the oldest language and Adam and Eve talked in it, and this weird old man named Enoch was the last person who knew it. I don't know how everyone suddenly stops remembering how to talk. What did they do, start talking Spanish one day instead?" She giggled, covering her mouth with her hand.

She petted Dog's ears, lifting one to whisper in more intimately. "I was taught this morning how to use special Enochian words as a key to unlock a secret room down the hall. It's amazing. You wouldn't even know the door was there! I learned all about how to do my new job." Holding Dog, she opened her other arm out wide to illustrate the grandeur and hit the man next to her in the cheek with the wet sucker. She apologized and said, "I'm sorry, I don't have anything to clean it off with. Should I lick the sticky off?"

The man smiled, gently shook his head, spit on his sleeve and wiped it off. Crank got up and said, "Now is the time to reach deep into your pockets and give to the Bible fund. We all have heard about that terrible country with the President rumored to be *Home Oh! Sex U All.*" He paused between each syllable, with a toothy grin. "Can you imagine how much the people living here need to hear the Word? How can they think that's all right with the Lord? As you all know, we're sending a truckload of Bibles there, and that's expensive for common folk such as us. So dig deep, brothers and sisters. Dig deep."

Emily returned to whispering to Dog. "I practiced and practiced because if I do anything wrong, really bad, bad things happen. Lots badder than what just now happened. I don't know what. I can do my job on my own next time all by myself. And you know what? They're going to give me the best presents ever after every day I do that job. I can't wait to see what they are. But, don't worry. You'll always be my favorite toy. Maybe I can sneak you into the secret room sometime. You should see it. It's very, very, very strange." She shook her head at him and pursed her lips, widening her eyes even more. She kicked the seat in front of her by mistake and slouched down, carrying Dog down lower into the pew.

She continued, "I'm sorry I haven't explained things to you enough. I should talk to you more, shouldn't I, sweetie? You see, this is how it works. Isis is the queenie. The king chess piece is a silly Egyptian man, Osiris, holding a crook. And out of his death, a flamingo named Bennu was borned. I know it's complicated. I'm probably the only little girl in the country who knows anything about it! You see, they're the same thing: Osiris and the flamingo god. That's what they showed me, in the play. The members of the … socicity?

Um… *society* like to do the play a lot, even though everyone already knows it by heart. It's kind of boring. I don't know why they don't do something new. That's always funner, don't you think, Dog?"

Emily shook her hair and blinked her large green eyes in rhythm to the glossolalia. She watched Martha raise her hand awkwardly above her right hip, the woman holding a cell phone with the camera pointing toward Crank. She clicked it, the flash landing on Crank's eyes, which were closed in apparent ecstasy as he spoke in tongues. Martha then sneaked the phone back into a pocket in her long full skirt before Crank's ice-blue eyes opened. She looked around, frowning. When her eyes met Emily's, Martha pursed her lips and turned away.

Emily went *tsk, tsk tsk*, shaking her head. She wagged her finger at the side of Martha's head. "The demons are going to get you," she whispered.

The pianist started playing a simple melody with one finger at a time on the upright piano. "It's our song," Emily said to Dog, jiggling the toy. Dog's head bounced, as if in agreement, on the spring.

Emily remembered everything the deacon said about the poison, each nuance, alternating between one and two syllable words. She memorized the Enochian words he said, automatically without thinking about it at all, her eyes unblinking, her head nodding in rhythm.

She knew what she had to do.

It was her move.

CHAPTER FIVE
Angela Ageless

Later that night, several blocks from the church, Angela Ageless slid her hand under the hem of her slinky black dress and played with the smoothness so slowly she successfully caught the NFL quarterback, Rios', attention from across the dimly lit hotel room. She tossed her long, curly auburn wig and snarled like a stunning, very female slender Elvis, raising her lips, in a look that entranced men. Martha had taught her the ways of seduction well over the years. Very well. She felt good with her darkly painted eyebrows and her usual temporary tattoo of a butterfly on her cheek. She *inhabited* the seductive fingers moving with entrancing slowness across her dress, as Rios watched in silence, unmoving.

"Damn, woman!" said one of the other football players hanging out in the suite. "Watchoo doing here?"

"It's Saturday night, isn't it? Well, then. Making the night *sing*."

"Zing, zing. Well, use a little of that vibrato on me," said the man, taking an exaggerated breath, grinning, and nodding down at his pelvis. He was wearing a silk robe, barely tied together.

Angela smirked at him and walked toward Rios with loose hips and fluid motion.

"What do you say we get this party started," she said, lifting one side of her heavily garnet-lipsticked mouth. "You don't come through our fine city often enough for us to waste any time getting down to business. I missed you, babies." She looked over at Rios. "Especially you, chico." She handed the other football player a drug. Such a simple pill, which he took from her hand casually. Yet did he ever think about how it had been transported in the corpses of soldiers sent home from the last country where the Agents of the Nevermind had created a coup in the country next to his? She wanted to slap him, make him grow up and think about reality. But no, her job was to make him forget.

The other men in the room came around, and she passed the street drugs out, while moving into the most alluring poses. One grabbed her and held her to him, while he took the illicit substances.

"Did everyone get your - *beer*?" she asked, sneering as she looked upward indicating a hidden microphone in the gilded molding along the indigo ceiling. She loudly emphasized the lie that she was only giving them alcohol, lowering her false eyelashes.

She and everyone else knew to be careful what was said in the room: all the hotels the football players stayed in were bugged during their stint there. The team's owners had to be able to come up with proof if someone was messing with the team, if they were doing drugs, or anything along those lines. But at most places they could have a reasonably legal good time. That was expected.

She went up to Rios, and pulled him onto the bed, rumpling the golden silk sheets. When he hesitated, looking around, she said, "Who cares who watches?" she asked. "I don't. Do you? Are you a wuss?" She slid her hand along his growing crotch.

Tantra Bensko

"Nah, that's quite OK. You feel free to go right ahead with what you're doing."

They took off their clothes, sliding their hands over each other, pressing themselves together, growing moist and heated, throbbing together. She made him feel good. Real good. Other football players in the room stole glances, cheered and leered, then openly abandoned their conversations one by one, breathing heavily. Eventually, all but his roommate left. The roommate went to bed and turned off the lights, and said, "Thank you, mystery lady, for the good shit. You know we'll never tell on you, ever. You're our favorite bitchessa in the city. Night."

She knew exactly what Rios liked, kinky as it was. She pushed his hand away when he tried to give her an orgasm. That didn't matter. She wasn't there for her own pleasure. What mattered was how he felt, and she put all of her skills into making sure he was pleased as he could be. She exhausted him, and she yelled out in the exposed display of lust. The roommate tossed and turned, sighing audibly across the room.

She and Rios lay there resting awhile after sex, and then she pulled on her clothes luxuriously, her pale, toned legs pointed up in the air. She stretched feet, aiming her toes at the light above them. Blood pulsing through her veins and breathing so deeply felt good. She'd sweated out impurities, and she was mostly through with her job. She gave herself the luxury of fantasizing about being with a man who accepted her for what she was, hollow and ruthless as that had to be in order to protect the banks of Americans everywhere.

She wished, with all her heart, she could have just had regular sex with Rios and all the other men in the past, just because she liked them. And when she felt like it. Not because they were marks.

56

Rios was dangerous to the stability of the U.S. economic system, which was financially dependent on endless war. He brought too much positive attention to the President of his country, who was, like the other unfortunate leaders the U.S. had brought down, creating a happy country that would make people in the U.S. question how their own country had to be run. If that President followed through on the plans of independence on imports and the petrodollar, people in the U.S. would need to downgrade their lifestyles to accommodate the shift.

Or, on the other hand, Rios was exactly what the U.S. needed. The difference hinged entirely on how well his subconscious reacted to what she was about to program into it by using the ancient occult secret espionage code. She leaned to his ear, kissing and nibbling it. As she did, she softly sang the Enochian call designed to trigger him without him realizing it, slowly, one syllable at a time.

She jumped back when he said, "What are you doing? You wacko? Don't be coming around doing that weird shit."

"Oh really?" She hid her surprise and purred, placing her hand firmly on his crotch. "Never again? You're sure about that?"

His penis was already hard again. He'd do exactly what she'd programmed his mind to do when she spoke Enochian, she was sure. *He* just didn't consciously know he would, which was all for the best. She was well aware that he'd been abducted in the past and gone through the Enochian call and response programming during the nights he remembered only strange dreams of Osiris Slain turning into Osiris Risen. She knew. She was there. The Scarlet Woman of espionage would *always* be there.

The halftime show at the Super Bowl would trigger his programming. Not only his but everyone else's, as long as he accompanied it with the right football plays, mathematically reversing and traversing, acting out the mysteries encoded in the esoteric tables and charts. His patterns of movement would deepen the post-hypnotic suggestions in all the split-agents, all the couriers, all the slaves, all the assassins, all the Manchurian Candidates and moles who didn't know what they were doing. If Rios got the plays wrong, their programming could degrade too.

Rios was a famous and very vocal supporter of the current President in his country. Obviously, such a cult figure couldn't be allowed to do well in football any longer. Football fans would start to admire his President instead of hate him and that would make the underhanded destruction of that country less popular. Even activists in the U.S. were finally realizing how beneficial the President was to his country... They agitated, wanting to see the U.S. become similar. Activists arguing with soldiers joining up... Students threw themselves at the police when protesting the Nevermind recruiting on campus. They boycotted Ehroh video games with that President as the antagonist.

Even more people in his country would get behind his cause, if Rios kept winning games. Rios had to be made to look stupid. Angela had been tasked by the Nevermind Agency with seeing to that. The U.S. had enough trouble making that President look bad, as it was, without someone as charming as Rios traveling around stirring up positive sentiment toward the socialist-tinted regime.

But something went wrong. Rios grabbed her by the arm, twirling her around and said, "Wait. Hell. I remember you. Not just from our parties. No, no, no. Something entirely different. I remember a damn pink *bird*. A fucking flamingo! That wasn't a dream!"

Angela Ageless shushed him, looking around at the other players nervously. His programming was breaking down! Apparently she and Crank hadn't done a good enough job with the mind control training in the past. But Rios would be the one to be blamed. And so would she. Not just her but...

Rios' moves in the football game, which Emily had delivered to him through Enochian code, would be mimicked by the occult chess game underneath the President's room, in order to theoretically waft up the magick through the ceiling. The Bee of Ra must prevail.

She pushed Rios down on the bed, and leaving her umbrella there, ran breathless out into the night, melting in the rain into a puddle of forget.

CHAPTER SIX
Cryptic Messages

Sunday evening, Nancy's piano teacher left, after their first lesson in a year. He'd taken her smooth hands in his veiny ones as he sat next to her on the stool, and said, "Nancy, your playing is still on the thin side. I'd love to see you break your distance from the instrument. You need to lower your fingers with more feeling as if you're pressing below the surface of the keys. Send energy into the heart of the piano. More nuance. Put more of your true *self* into the pressure on the keys. *Be* more of yourself. Let the music express it. Let us feel it. The way it is, it sounds like you don't really *feel* who you are." His eyes penetrated hers deeply. She felt as if he was entering her soul. She wished she could do that with herself.

Nancy had quit their previous lessons just when she started making progress toward concert-quality emotion in her playing. Something about paying that much attention to her music brought little hints of those strange, dreamlike ideas about her past. She felt the stress of that much concentration made her start "remembering" things that made no sense.

Normally, she tried to stay on the surface of herself, just as her teacher said. Things seemed more logical that way. But

60

now, she was determined to get good at playing, even if it meant a little cognitive dissonance. Sunday nights were once again her accountability nights.

She took only half a Jolly. That would start the process of being able to make her way in life without her uncle. She played the "Moonlight Sonata" in her mind and slowly danced to it throughout her apartment. She turned on the bath water and lit a rose-scented candle in her bathroom; while she waited for the tub to fill, she popped over to a few social media sites, something she'd hardly taken the time to do for a while. She had a chance to do whatever she wanted. She'd spent time, in that weekend, in one of her blackouts, and she didn't want her life to get away from her.

She drank a cocktail, ready to put her feet up in a lavender bath littered with dried rose petals. She had to make time for herself to relax and stretch, instead of spending her conscious time thinking about the attack on the sidewalk Saturday morning, or she was going to burst.

She had no idea what had happened after being put into the strange car after she was made unconscious when she left Alyssa's place. They'd apparently used the key in her pocket when they brought her back home. But that meant they knew where she lived. She needed to change her lock once again.

Or had she sleepwalked home on her own? Just as likely.

She had to assume Geoff had hired someone to give her a more serious warning about the XXX, since she was continuing to sleuth around in his life. Maybe she was getting warmer with the waste management. What if other times, when she'd come into consciousness when sleepwalking in public, she'd also been abducted? By Geoff's goons. She blanched.

She wasn't about to go to the police with it. Not until she had solid proof. She hadn't seen more than the corner of the front bumper of the car. She'd come to consciousness as she usually did after her fugues. Reporting the event would give Geoff the perfect excuse to claim she was nuts. If Geoff was in the mob... didn't they pay off the police?

She suspected that if she told about her sporadic amnesia she'd be put in some horrible institution, slapped with a "crazy" label, and given nasty drugs. The Jollys Geoff gave her staved off the hallucinations. False memories. Whatever.

The book she'd stolen from Alyssa was no longer in her backpack. She remembered the author's name, but didn't want to look it up online. Nancy didn't want anyone remotely watching her searches. One harrowing abduction like that was enough warning for her.

She puzzled, again, over the strange scent she'd woken up with that morning. Like men's cologne. It was familiar, but she couldn't, or wouldn't, place it. All she knew was, it was uncomfortable not being in control of her life, suspecting every smell. She wanted to get rid of her problems with bergamot oil.

She hummed the song from her childhood that haunted her. She promised herself she'd finish composing it, make it richer, filled in with more layers like it used to be, would play it with both hands, her fingers deep in the soul of the music, adding in the depth of the low notes. She'd let the rest of it come to her in the bath. It so often almost did. Almost.

The phone rang unanswered. She turned away, as if it couldn't see her if she didn't look at it.

On her laptop, she saw a message from Jeff on social media, the man who had been writing the eccentric little quips to her on social media. Over the month, they'd been communicating more deeply. Everything was poetic, though annoyingly garbled. She'd opened her heart to him, enjoying what seemed to be a humble, self-deprecating spirit, his appreciation of her unusual qualities.

She had become put off by some of his messages to her and comments on his profile page, because they made no sense, though they were endearing, like something a developmentally disabled person or a child might write. They relentlessly related to what she'd just been doing at the time. Creepy. She tried to tell herself she was just seeing connections that weren't there. Life did have lots of synchronicities, after all. Being paranoid never made anyone any friends. Or, at least, not the kind anyone really wanted to have.

Maybe her dopamine was getting too high. Or maybe she'd eaten something that was prepared in a kitchen where they used gluten, and it had gotten contaminated. Even a few molecules could make her connect the dots and see constellations of meaning that weren't there. The circle on her neck was still red, though the welt was fading. Maybe she was having a lingering psychotic reaction to that offending protein.

It sure couldn't be what she felt like it was. Demonic possession. She knew how ridiculous that sounded. But, somehow, it seemed to be echoing in her head. Who could have given her that idea?

What if Jeff had the capacity to watch her searches online and respond to them in encoded messages?

Was his newest message a warning too? "Fly free my little wind-swept glee. Or come and sit down on my knee."

She turned the computer off. She put on a satin black eye-covering, blocking out the light to make her brain produce more melatonin, and she danced blind in her living room. She willed his messages to all be pure coincidence. She lifted her eye-covering when she noticed she was wearing a child's hair bow. She quickly slipped it off and let it fall to the floor. She had no idea what to think about that.

Tantra Bensko

After her luxurious bath, she put on a nightie and turned on the old-fashioned TV to relax that evening. She flipped around from channel to channel. She paused on a news report about the President of a country she had not given much thought to. The newscaster talked about how he had gained popular support in the past, but now was facing an aggressive uprising. There were scenes of mobs of people protesting against him, championing another option for a President they preferred to take his place. They were chanting in the streets and waving their fists, holding pictures of the man they wanted to win the next election.

She switched to a different station. She felt as if she couldn't help doing so. An announcer thanked the troops for tuning in from one hundred and seventy-five countries where they were stationed, in order to keep power over the populace. An advertisement, projected on a screen, showed a video game promoting the glories of war, put in terms of football. The Super Bowl was on, and the nation was watching. The NFL saluted the military with a presentation of colors, flyovers, guests talking about the promoted enemies of the moment. Military jets and helicopters protected the stadium.

The theme of the halftime show was children's imagination, and the ability to keep their dreams alive. If children wanted to be great sports players, they could, as long as they didn't give up on their fantasies. That belief apparently allowed people to perform spectacularly in their chosen field. The choreographed performance included children who could fly and disappear, point their fingers and make someone faint, talk to animals who talked back, and sing magical notes that made enemies into friends, and opposite team members become laughably terrible players.

The show mixed and matched characters from children's books that had been produced as movies by the Agents of the Nevermind, since their production company, Ehroh, bought Lookout Mountain Labs in Los Angeles. The children in the halftime show fought the fuddy-duddy adults who had lost their belief in doing the impossible, and who had only sensible weapons. The children were able to defeat the mundane weapons every time with their occult abilities.

A sponsor flag showed the symbol of a huge local library. It was known for esoterica, propaganda, and children's literature. It was rumored to be a front for the Agents of the Nevermind. The insignia displayed intimidating authority. Another sponsor was the Ehroh production company, which had made the edgy movie, *Emily Doesn't Mind*, from the children's book, *He Who Came into Being by Himself*, which featured a character named Emily, and Bennu, the flamingo of Osiris, based on the traditional belief that one could morph into the other. Osiris held the crook, which resembled a flamingo.

In the theatrical performance, Osiris chased the children, until they became proactive and ran at him, hiding under his apron. He did a magic trick in which he seemed to enlarge as he opened out his arms and his cloak expanded all around him, covering him momentarily. Suddenly, it flipped inside out and he became Bennu, ruffling his feathers and screeching.

Nancy cringed, cursed and pulled back into her loveseat when she watched the flamingo Bennu sing a hideous nonsense tune. Her stomach hurt. She'd heard that song before.

Children leapt into baskets, punted each other like footballs, and flew from one goal to another. They sat on the shoulders of the adults, covering their faces and giggling, spanking them to make them go forward. A little girl dressed as Emily from *Emily Doesn't Mind* sang, wearing a little black dress with a white collar and a jagged make-up arrow down the front of her face. Leering, Bennu followed Emily around as her brothers and sisters watched. He chased her into a closet, lifting his feathers at her ominously and poking his long beak inside.

When Bennu came out without Emily, he gathered up the smaller siblings, calming them down, telling them to be brave. She sang, "Don't worry. Davey and Pill will take you flying. Better than being in bed, or dying."

A pasty, disheveled man knocked on the door, and the children ran into their beds. The man leaned down to them to kiss them goodnight. As he sat there on Emily's bed, petting her, the children all lying down, other versions of the children appeared in white diaphanous gauze clothing, rising from behind them, with gold lights attached to their backs.

The gauzy versions of the children floated blankly out the window, apparently on pulleys, to follow their fantasy into some other world. The crowd cheered when the stage spun around and the little high triangular window was on the other side. The children flew, with the man, into the newly revealed room in that section of the round stage. The child playing Emily, from the children's story, was the first one to land.

In that room, a miniature football game was in progress. The children grabbed footballs that were flying in the air in a whimsical fashion and flew with them, landing in perfect positions to drop the balls into the hands required for their team to win the bizarre game of the midpoint in the real football game.

Nancy gasped as she watched. It was beautiful, in a macabre fairy tale way. But, watching the Emily character punished by Bennu was like being vicariously punished by her own personal boogie man. Or being warned that she would be. Well, *that* was ultimate paranoia. Why didn't she just think about shoes, and rock stars, and scoring a rich man, like other women her age?

She lay down across the couch. She reminisced about her youth, how she wrote all that fan fiction about being the Emily character from the movie, riding Bennu with mixed feelings, uncertainly flying through the sky. The angst of the flying made her sleep so hard in the past that when she landed, everything was sweet and fine. She'd never thought about those stories much in her adult life, but had only chuckled nostalgically thinking of what an imagination she had back then, what a loyal fan she was of Emily, how she identified with her. She tried to remember the stories but, for the first time in her life, realized – there *were* no stories.

She didn't actually write any. Not one.

She'd just always told herself that she did. Instead, she *lived* the stories, whatever they were. But what could that possibly mean?

A tear rolled down her face. All her capillaries felt like they were constricting at once. She usually fought off the visions that came when she didn't take a full Jolly. But this time, she tried to remember what she'd lived and forgotten, closing her eyes, putting her head down… Her uncle rubbing his upper thighs with a hand under the table, at dinner. He'd move his fingers back and forth repetitively against his pants, and she would turn her head away, nauseated. He'd then move his finger in and out of his mouth, sliding it across his full lips, as he sat at the table.

Then, the usual images came up that made her lose her train of thought when she tried to tune into what seemed to be more important than those surface memories. Intersected upward and downward triangles flashed, spinning, and reversing colors, black and white, pulsing, forming a tunnel that pulled her into it, the sound like a train overwhelming her like a black hole, like nothing.

She didn't know how, but she suddenly knew the way she felt had something to do with Bennu. It was the fake memories again that had kept her taking the pills year after year to stave them off. Still, they didn't exactly feel false. There was something in her past that she was supposed to remember, just enough to forget, to forget just enough to remember. The flamingo was some kind of menace beyond just a children's story. Bennu left his trace everywhere.

No, it was just dreams she'd had. It had to be. She had an active imagination, especially when she was asleep. She remembered dreams of him coming into her room at night. Teaching her to fly into another world, through a window, where everything was an adventure. A terrible taste. A syringe.

She remembered a strange scene from a dream she'd had during the night. She lay down and curled over, pulling a black silk covering over her eyes, to help her remember more. She and her brothers and sisters she often dreamed about, yet didn't actually have, were in their bedroom, bouncing on their beds. Everything was in black and white.

In the dream, a man came in, wearing an overly large pink suit and strange curvy hat that came down over his face in a point, and they all tangled up together. She didn't remember what it was that hurt. She remembered them all gathering by the window in awe. The man flapped his suit like wings, and flew out the window in the dream, and as he left, his head, neck, shoulders, and progressively his whole body became colored in as it crossed the window.

The world outside their house became intense and saturated with glorious color. Inside, just dull grays. The children followed him out, flying, and all became colorized too. What did they do out there, she wondered, in the other world that she forgot?

68

Once, when she was very young, she'd shown her father a suspicious needle mark on her arm in the morning and he had laughed. "Mosquitos are bad this time of year," he'd said. "I should spray the house. Time to call Geoff and get the good ol' family discount." She'd thrown a tantrum, and he'd made her go to her room.

She turned her attention to the TV again. The giant papier-mâché Bennu on the halftime show, larger than life, chased the little girl playing the role of Emily to punish her. She had misbehaved, and must be corrected. He raised her to the sky calling down the sky gods to come and devour her. He held the young girl up feet first, then grasped her around the pelvis. Nancy could hardly stand to look at the screen. She could feel threat in her body.

The little actress covered up one eye with her hand and opened her first and second fingers to make a triangle, the traditional "illuminati sex-slave" symbol. The girl's black bangs separated in hard lines above it, echoing the triangle and intersecting with it. It was like the D-CIDE logo. And, like Terry Crank's logo reversed and spinning, spinning into the dark. Like the two of them combined, like the portal to doom.

When Nancy saw that, she completely forgot the dreams she had just begun to remember.

It was Nevermind time.

She'd liked watching TV with her father, mostly cartoons. Even when he watched sports, it was fun to sit in his lap when she was little. When the teams he liked won, he'd bounce her and tickle her. Nancy's mother once gave her a balloon printed with the name of her home team that was playing that weekend and she'd carried it everywhere, even when it had deflated. She missed her parents. She cuddled a pillow on the couch.

Her uncle had always gotten excited, too, when he watched football games, when Nancy had lived with him. Sure, a lot of people watching games act like they won them themselves. He was different. He'd be cool about it, but the gleam in his eye was too bright. She pulled herself back into one piece the best she could immediately, but felt as if that moment was some sort of window. A portal she flew through into another, more colorful world for an instant. A world in which football really, really mattered. More than rationality suggested it should matter. As if she would die if something went wrong with the game. As if it would be her fault if it did.

And he'd brought up the words "million dollars" during the games, sweating so much he stank up the house. After a big game like the Super Bowl, he'd be in a great mood, hugging her, kissing her cheeks, and congratulating her as if she was the one who had won the game. Even his friends had done that. Carrying her on their shoulders and giving her treats. One said she was their little good luck charm. She'd smiled up at him, and he'd patted her on the bottom.

But, even though they'd joke about making lots of money from the game, their family never got millions of dollars richer, that Nancy could tell. When she'd asked her uncle for a horse, since she'd made them win the game by being a good luck charm, he'd told her the money he won was used to fund something bigger than their family. More important. Something secret that he couldn't talk about. And, he told her, if she talked about him betting on the game, he'd have to abandon her to the streets and how would she like that?

Streets were dirty and cold. She didn't want to live there forever.

She massaged her abdomen and stretched uncomfortably. She had to admit she really did feel some

70

pain and bloating in her pelvis. It seemed like a bladder infection coming on. She couldn't keep denying it. Sugar was only making it worse. She pondered how that could be the case, as infections only happened to her after she had sex. But she hadn't had sex. Had she? She went to the kitchen and drank some cranberry juice she kept on hand.

When the game started up again after the imagination-themed halftime, Nancy stared at the set in her living room. Her eyes darted around, identifying the sidelines and end lines, yard lines and goal lines. She watched the referee's coin toss. She knew something was intensely important, but she didn't know what. She counted eleven players on a team, until her eyes landed on the quarterback.

She felt as if she knew the dark-haired man, somehow, as if she had met him recently. Maybe just at a party or something. Maybe not. She didn't remember going to any parties. The game was being broadcast live from not far away in the city. Maybe she'd just passed him on the street. She threw her cup on the floor and stared at the wet spot.

It mattered intensely to her how the game turned out. Her quarterback's team was on the offense. The hair stood up on her arms as she watched the advancing of the ball toward the end zone. They didn't even gain ten yards, couldn't even get to a first down, and something about that seemed vital to her wellbeing.

The fascia tightened along her upper arms, the temperature of her skin changing. She couldn't tell if it was hot or cold. She was supposed to do something of utmost importance. What? It was too late, but she couldn't help rooting the offensive team on, even though she cared nothing for sports. She yelled at the TV and waved her fist. Her stomach twisted up, and she curled over.

She got a call on her landline. She didn't know if she should answer. It rang on. She bit her fingernails and cut into her lip, swearing and dabbing at the blood with her cigarette butt.

How could she have met the quarterback, who was apparently called Rios? The voices narrating the game talked about him often, with shock and disappointment in their voices.

She shook her head and sang her favorite songs that usually made everything seem homey and predictable. Then, she realized she'd seen Rios on the news a few months back when he was talking about how great the President was in his home country.

That might have even been why the segment about the riots was on the news at the same time as the Super Bowl. The President was a favorite among people who believed in independence and honest transparency and free health care and guarantees of housing. *That* was why Nancy recognized the quarterback. She was relieved it was something so normal. He was a celebrity among activists who believed positive government was possible. *Whew.*

His beloved President had created an irrigation project and made water available to everyone, along with free livestock, money for mothers, and electricity. And he was about to create a State Bank, with no external debt and no interest on loans. He was preparing to launch a new independent currency based on gold.

The game didn't seem to be going well. Rios looked lost. The referee was shouting at him. Some men in expensive suits sat palpably still behind him, leaning forward, watching him with their lips tight and straight across.

"Throw it! Throw the game!" she yelled. The phone rang again. She threw a pillow at it, which muffled the noise slightly. "Come on, Rios!" She tried to will him to screw up the pass.

She rooted with all her might for the opposing team to win. Rios made one bad move after another. He fumbled and ran slowly, passed poorly, and was easily intercepted. He caused infractions.

But then he took a time out and crouched in the corner, with his head in his hands. He pushed people away when they talked to him. Then, he suddenly got up and set his jaw and returned to the field; he stood up straighter and strode with purpose.

He played with panache and smooth movements he hadn't been exhibiting earlier that evening. He kept scoring, scoring, scoring, as was expected, considering he was the star player on the team. The crowd stood up and shouted, encouraging the sudden turnaround. His team recovered points. More touchdowns, kickoffs, touchdowns, kickoffs.

His team was ultimately victorious. The crowd went wild.

Something loosened in her. Something that was supposed to tighten by watching the game, screwing down her programming deeper inside.

Signaling the end of the game, one flag was taken down and another put up. Her head fell against her shoulder immediately, and she was asleep. Everything she had just remembered would fade like a dream.

When she woke up, she turned off the TV, not sure why she'd subjected herself to watching a game she had no interest in. She'd never cared for spectator sports. She liked the exercise of playing sports, like tennis, but saw no benefit from watching someone else get a workout. She contemplated what seemed like a dream about wanting a particular football player to lose, for some reason. "Huh. I never thought I'd dream about someone like that. Football! Of all things."

73

She stretched and yawned, and put on some music. She was glad to be alive.

She remembered she had to find a new job so she never had to see Geoff again. She'd worked in a water bottling plant during the short phase when she tried to be free of D-CIDE, but they'd fired her when she didn't come in too many days she spent blacked out. *That was fifteen years ago, so maybe they've forgotten all about me and trashed the old records. It can't hurt to try.* It wasn't much of an upgrade from a company that killed pests. It glorified plastics and was actually the same as tap water, just not as carefully regulated. It stole water from one place and sent it to other places for profit, and added fluoride to it, which made people's thyroids work poorly.

She imagined instead living in nature by a spring, deer drinking from it, and of course, Julio lying with her naked on the green, green moss. She'd play with his heavy hair, and run her hand down his body. Music would be playing in the air, somehow.

That meant she had to first quit the pills. *Withdrawals.* No dependence on Geoff. *Geoff, what a stupid name, anyway.*

If he knew she was the one trying to report the dumping, and if it was him who had sent some goons to throw her in a car, she had to find a job in some other state — without job referrals. She had to pack to be ready in case. She fantasized about a witness protection program. *I wonder how I'd look in a curly black wig. I should get fat. Paint moles all over my face.*

She preferred to stay in denial as long as she could, and to see Julio again. But, should she take the chance? She had to clean the house and give notice of moving away.

Hearing her laptop ding, she knew someone had just sent her a message on social media. She hoped it was something comforting. She could use some oxytocin. She walked over to the desk and noticed something new: a friend request sitting there - from her uncle Geoff. No! No! Too close for comfort!

But that wasn't the worst of it. The ding had actually been alerting her to a creepy new message. From Jeff: "Nothing works. It's just a play. It didn't turn out right. You are supposed to obey."

What? What kind of a freaky poem is that?

She jiggled her foot and reached over for a mini-candy bar, tearing the wrapper only partly off while she looked at the screen. She bit into the wrapper by mistake, and chewed it up, spitting it out on the floor. The more she thought about the statement, the more her skin felt as if it were a plastic wrapper. A tight one. Getting tighter. Suffocating her.

The message from Jeff continued: "I mean. You have just go with flow. Humans have screwed up planetary by being brain. Let it carbry."

"Carbry?"

"Tomorrow, going be there."

"Where?"

"HA. You don't know where you are? I'll bring book."

"I don't have room to put you up." She didn't know what to say. How to keep him from coming into her apartment? "And my place is kind of messy...."

"No prob, a bird just flew by. Cubicle city of beds will work for me."

The top of her head seemed like it was starting to spin in both ways at once, and molecules of thoughts were flying off in all directions. "So, I guess we should get together? What time? I'm off tomorrow because D-CIDE always observes the American Sports Holiday."

"Noon. Moon Cafe by your place. Soon. The road will never grow old."

How did he know where she lived? God, she hated that kind of thing. She ate another mini-candy bar. Then, she went into the kitchen and balanced it out with a beauty salad she put together quickly. Ruby red tomatoes, raw sauerkraut, sprouts and olive oil. She inhaled it.

She assumed he was just tuned into the synchronistic nature of the universe, but still. Fucking still. That cryptic message felt claustrophobic. She couldn't help it. She read more online, searching for information about the evangelical group run by Reverend Crank. Nothing was coming up with her searches, just the official praising and whitewashing. Page twelve, page thirteen, nothing to tell her anything useful at all, nothing that confirmed what Alyssa had said.

She started to turn off the computer but decided to try one more page. Page fourteen was the definite winner. There was plenty of dirt on Crank there, and in the following pages, though his supporters would have closed their eyes to the articles by independent journalists.

Brandon's video, she had to admit, was the best: "Crank's organization promotes going to war with non-Christians in other countries and has a solid presence in the United Nations. They send aid to horrible U.S.-backed groups overthrowing popular and successful elected Presidents. Its head missionaries are rumored to be members of the Nevermind working with the Army chaplains. What are they doing? Apparently spying on the people in the countries where they travel, as well as infiltrating local activist organizations. Yes, maybe yours. Members of a certain branch pretend to be counterculture types to persuade the hip young people to vote for their favored Christian politicians in order to pass laws the Agents want. They are not known to be pious.

"They combine forces with FEMA to identify which people are easily manipulated by cults. For historical context, you might want to watch my earlier video about how the Bee of Ra's original leader eventually became the first head of the Nevermind."

"Oh, it's all about you, isn't it?" Nancy asked his smugly animated image.

His video voice talked over her. "The Agents send the most gullible people to where they want them. They experiment on them. They set up cult leaders to tell devotees to spy for the Agents for free. Seriously, Crank is Man of the Year: our most admired American. The epitome of the trusted religious leader archetype. But dig below the surface, folks. You don't have to search far to find the hypocrisy."

She knew her uncle went away on church-related trips sometimes, but she'd thought they probably went canoeing or something. She'd had no idea what denomination he was. She'd assumed he just pretended to be pious to meet women.

Brandon did call-in radio interviews and did videos with slide shows, but never showed his face. She wondered what he looked like. The rumor was he was an HGH giant, as there were a few giants still around after the surge of artificially created gigantism in the early 90's when *Giant Jack* comics were all the rage and people were getting into the ancient Atlantis root race mythology big time.

The illegal dumping was the kind of thing Brandon needed to talk about sometime on his video channel, in her opinion. It was right up his alley. She wondered if she should contact him. She'd have to hide her identity, start a new account from a library, so no one could track her.

She flipped through social media. Checked through what her friends had been posting, normal things, happy things. She took a deep breath. She started to post something silly about cats. She just didn't know what. *Something*. And then, she got another message from Jeff about coming to visit right away.

She responded: "Why are you coming here?"

Tantra Bensko

There was no answer. Her stomach tensed. *Is someone logging my keystrokes? Watching my searches? Is Jeff a warning sent to me to prevent me from reporting the XXX crime?*

That horrible thought made her sit, put her head down on the desk, close her eyes tightly, and sob.

CHAPTER SEVEN
The Coffee Shop

Monday morning and Jeff still hadn't answered.

Nancy went for a run through the neighborhood, passing by her favorite Victorian house, with an orange turret and an old hobby horse stuck on top of the iron fence. Monday was one of her days off that week, and instead of spending it mysteriously blacked out, she was glad to inhabit her awakening. She admired how shapely her calves were from so much exercise. She looked down at her firm thighs when she crossed a street. She was fast. She had endurance. *I'm a rad chick. I'll be OK.*

She circled back, and as she neared her apartment, she heard the wonderful sound of the first house finches of the season and flashed back to when a man from the service branch of D-CIDE had come out to the house when she was at elementary school. When she'd gotten home, she'd tugged at his sleeve and asked the serviceman, "Why are you here this time?"

"I took care of the attic. There were *finches* in there."

"You didn't hurt them, did you?"

"They were breeding!"

"What did you do?"

He'd hesitated, wrinkling his forehead and breathing through his mouth, with bad breath. "Don't worry. I put them on the ground, and their mothers came and got them."

She'd been relieved. Until days later, when the feeling crept up on her. He'd done nothing of the kind. He'd fooled her once again: telling her a story to make her fuzz out about the reality of life and death.

And then, one week later exactly, when she walked out of her house, dead finches were laid out in a diorama. The males formed an upward pointing triangle and the females formed a downward triangle. She'd grabbed her stomach, closed her eyes and ended up in her Special Place. The mental state she went into when she was too traumatized to stay normal. How could she have trusted the operator, after he'd tricked her into horror so often?

When she got home from her run, she drank water from one of her tarnished pewter goblets that made her feel special and timeless. She showered, opening her mouth, like a bird in the rain, dried and braided her hair, put on an adventurous outfit, and before long, set off walking with a deliberately jaunty step, to the coffee house on the corner to meet Jeff.

She needed to get a grip on herself. Her stomach was uneasy, thinking again about how his strange little remarks so often related to exactly the obscure things she was looking up online. She walked the short block to the coffeehouse, saying hello to the people she passed, twittering at the songbirds, and patting the bark of a large sycamore by the sidewalk.

She saw her long-distance friend sitting at the outdoor table, already drinking tea. She recognized his black beret and wisps of prematurely graying hair sticking out from underneath it from his social media profile photo. "Hi, Jeff." She wondered if the gray was maybe just natural and he was older than he looked. His outfit looked like he was still trying

80

for a youthful appearance, but it was reminiscent of the suave city style from a hundred years ago. He looked out of place, but maybe that was because her vision was making his edges waver and flash.

He turned around and stood up to shake her hand. He reached out; she looked down and saw it. His right hand was a curved glistening sharp *hook* carved into the shape of a fucking *flamingo*.

Ahhhh!

Her legs gave way for a split second, and her hand shook when she reached out to grasp onto the cold steel. She felt as if she had a fever. He was not smiling. He looked as if he had never smiled in his life.

"Good to meet you in person, Nancy. You look younger than you do in your photos. So youthful. Like you'll never ever grow up. Never grow up."

"You look - different, too. Not exactly how I thought you would." Her mouth was doing something on its own she couldn't keep control of. Like talking. Curling in. Trembling. "I'm so thirsty, all of a sudden. I'm going to go in and get some tea."

She stood in line for tea with a woman holding a crying baby in front of her. She wanted to cover her ears. She thought about hiding in the bathroom until the blood rose to her head again.

There was something from her childhood she didn't understand and it didn't just come from listening to the soundtrack of the story about Bennu. Something more visceral. Not dreams. Though it seemed like dreams. Not real. It didn't seem real. Something in between.

But she had been raised to stay polite. Mature. Keep calm. Count to ten, to force herself to stop crying, and get hold of herself. Finally, she ordered, asking for a kind of tea she hated, by mistake. She spilled the hot tea on herself and put in salt instead of sugar. She took it outside and drank it anyway, grimacing. She had never had so many drinks spill in her life as she had recently. "So, how has your trip been?"

"I've been seeing great landscapes and taking videos of them. I'm used to flying around here and there. I love the sky when the clouds are cumulus, don't you? Especially in the sunset or sunrise and they all turn colors, but especially, pink. Gorgeous, just gorgeous."

"Flying in planes, I take it."

"Oh, no, of course not," he said.

She watched the thin corners of his mouth closely. The creases folded into his jowls sharply. She couldn't tell where his smile would begin if he had one.

"Are you on vacation?"

"I've been sent on a mission at work."

"And that's for Pegasus International?"

"'We store your information in the cloud. So you don't have to remember anything ever again.'"

Such a dry wit. She grinned even more broadly at his quote from the company. She'd seen it when she'd clicked on the link on his social media page. But, his mouth didn't budge in any attempt to match her joviality.

"What do you do exactly?"

"I record people's lives in video. Your kids can look back on it. Some people use it on their business websites."

He pulled out his expensive video camera and opened the door, pressing playback. He'd uploaded a professionally edited piece with a swelling musical score. She didn't see any credits other than the PI sitting on a pink cloud, their logo. A spaced-out woman in the video was teaching a class on meditation. "Just forget your story," she suggested, her eyes closed in bliss, accompanied by sitar.

To Nancy's eyes, her pajama pants and loose top, covered with a shawl, looked gray, but people always called

82

that cult's uniform sky blue. Just like Martha's notebook she always wrote in that looked gray to Nancy but everyone else called blue. The teacher continued: "Let go of your ego. Let go of your need to control. Surrender. You are only spirit. Your body doesn't matter. Everyone you blame came here for a reason to play a role. Forgive them for anything. Don't hold onto your suffering. Forget, forget. As you burn off your karma, you'll be free like me."

Jeff flipped the camera door shut and rolled a knob along the side. He turned on Nancy and pressed a button to start recording.

"Am I supposed to be paying you for recording a video of me or something? Or is someone *else* paying you?"

"You're an interesting person. This is your spotlight. Reveal all."

"What?"

"Tell the world about your life. Were you ever married? Where did you grow up? How long did you take drugs? Are psychedelics the best way to set yourself free?"

"*What?* Why do you ask?" She was flabbergasted. The first time she'd seen photos of LSD tabs they'd looked familiar to her as something she was given as a toddler. She decided they were probably tiny rectangles of flattened bread called "the host." It seemed like it happened in a church with men wearing priestly robes, so it must have been. She tried to remember if her parents had ever talked to her about religion when she was little.

"Because I've got this book to give you." He reached into his backpack, taking things out one by one with his hook that opened its sharp point, dividing into two, like curved inflexible claws.

"What's the book about?"

"Your man."

"My man?"

83

"The psychedelic king." Jeff lifted his chin in solute.

"What makes you think I did psychedelics? My man? Why is he my man? What are you talking about? Hey, are you recording?" Was he trying to entrap her? Who would he give the recording to? Who was he really working for? Was this an attempt at blackmail?

"Yes."

"Turn it off, Jeff. I don't know what man you mean."

"Timothy Leary! I'm going to make a documentary about him, and how he's influenced a nation to be more mystical. His writing style is just great." Jeff's eyes shone.

"He's not my man at all. I know he was a mixed bag. I mean, I like Karen Horney, the psychiatrist whose work he built some of his social theories from. But, how are you going to reconcile the problems he caused by being part of MKULTRA and getting so many activists to tune out and go off their paths?"

"You're saying you don't like Leary?"

"Not really. Because I don't align myself with the CIA. Fucking drug-runners. I've never done any street drugs in my life." She put the Jollys out of her mind so she could look convincing. She wanted one. She fantasized about running to the bathroom and popping an extra pill. She started to sweat. How would she handle life without them?

She had a sense of what psychedelic visions were like, though she didn't know why, and they frightened her to no end. She knew there were two sides to the Leary story and acknowledged that she wasn't actually there when it all went down. She understood that Jeff could reasonably counter her argument and make some claim that Leary had at least some redeeming qualities.

Why am I so adamant about a casual conversation about a random dead person? I don't even care that much about things like that. That's Alyssa's territory. And that know-it-all, Brandon. Alyssa probably wouldn't care about all that boring silly conspiracy stuff he talks about, except she has the hots for him. The hots for making other people feel inferior because she watched every video Brandon ever fucking made.

Jeff said, still recording, "Leary got arrested and put in prison for drugs. How could he be dancing with the CIA? He was for freedom. They don't put rebels on the paycheck and kick them out of school and into prison." He looked at her as if to say, "duh." Yet, there was another layer she couldn't read in his face. His ice-blue eyes looked into hers with tiny pupils though the light outside was soft.

The illogic mixed with logic made her head feel like it was going to explode. "Well, of *course* he was related to the program. He's completely *core* to the MKULTRA project. What do you mean? He was useful in prison. MKULTRA Subproject 58 popularized LSD after testing it on him. And think about it – a lot of people ended up in prison because of his profiling method that police and security agencies use. Remember how colleges gave out free MMPI tests left and right? Leary said you could predict what someone might do in the future from the answers. He made the goddamn entry exam for the CIA."

"Ha, ha. Well, everyone can think what they want." He put down the camera and lifted his tea, using the hook and the backward hand on either side of the unsteady cup.

"A lot of activists dropped out because of idolizing people like him and Kesey, who was distributing LSD for the CIA too. And The Grateful Dead and Ram Dass and Ginsberg. They all had great qualities, I know. It's not my kind of music. I like classical. But people say they were amazing artists. Still, you can't leave out the true history and romanticize that time. Gottlieb helped them get LSD, for fuck's sake. You know, the head of the CIA. I'm not saying you shouldn't make a movie about him. But, you can't just leave something so major out of his biography."

"Why do you care so much? Why not just drink tea and laugh with your well-met old friend, eh, lady?" His metal glasses caught the sunlight, flashing painfully into her eyes.

She didn't know the answer. The more Jeff obstinately refused to listen to the facts she mentioned about the well-known program, but just kept talking, the more it felt like aggression. A challenge, a slap in the face. Jeff laughed dismissively.

He balanced his flamingo-shaped hook to hold the fork. Asking first subtly with a nod, she helped pull the paper off his straw and put it in his water for him. She tried to imagine how many trips it must have taken him to carry everything to the table before she got there, and how he must grow weary of having to balance everything with such difficulty. She tried to just feel compassion instead of wanting to knock sense into him.

He asked, "Are you trying to impress me with your smarts or something? You're so cute. You've got the prettiest little face I've ever seen in my life. Isn't that enough for you? Are you trying to act like a Harvard graduate too, missy?"

"Weirdo. Feminism happened, by the way."

"Oh, did it now?" He intoned that sentence as if talking to a kitten.

Nancy pushed through his condescension. "By the way, the other CIA guys, Wasson, and McKenna were in the social relations department at Harvard along with Leary. Which is where MK-ULTRA came from at that time. And the program learned their methods from the Paperclip scientists after WWII. In other words, Nazis. You know, like hypnosis. Mind control. All the stuff the Nevermind Agency does since they took that over from the CIA back in the 80's." She watched his face for signs.

"Ah, just forget about all that mind control stuff." He reached out with his hook and set it down hard enough by her on the table her tea cup rattled in its dish.

"What about -"

He laughed. "Yeah, right. Forget it."

She asked, "Did you turn off the recording?"

"No."

She fumed. She wanted to knock the camera off the table. Who was paying him to spy on her, to try to catch her up? Was it the Agents? What the hell? She watched his weathered face, continuing a forced smile, trying to see if he had a smile in him, but it was all frown. Was he playing with her emotions? How could he refuse to understand their importance? How could he be so ruthlessly insistent about dismissing the facts? She was flustered by her need to keep trying to convince him, when she just wanted to have a nice, casual conversation with a friend. She didn't like people looking at her funny in the coffee shop which was only a block from her house. All the people who worked there knew her name.

A coffee shop wasn't the place to let an ordinary discussion between two people casually getting to know each other get heated over a disagreement about someone's biography. No place was. Getting worked up about that was silly. Lots of people admired Leary. He was a likable guy. It was just an obscure subject from the past that had nothing to do with her. She kicked her foot underneath the table and took a deep breath.

She rolled a question around in her mouth. Was Jeff working for the Agents of the Nevermind? But what would they possibly want with her? She pushed the thought down, along with the anger. She burped in reaction. But, try as she might, she couldn't help obsessing over the strange messages he'd sent. Were they really passed to him from the

Nevermind in order to gaslight her? To make her seem crazy to the outside world - or to literally go completely insane.

As if she wasn't, already.

Did an Agent somehow know about her love/hate nightmares about Bennu? No, no, that was ridiculous. Bennu and the Emily character were regaining popularity, with the new movie in the making, so it was normal for women to pay attention to those figures, and the Nevermind Agency would know that, especially as movie-related merchandise was starting to pop up at stores. *No, it's just a coincidence.* Nancy counted to ten again.

Did the Agents send Jeff to terrify me because he's so much like Bennu? Am I being warned by a fucking flamingo, because I was going to bring attention to waste management? Is Jeff here because I dug into Geoff's connection with Crank's CIA and the Nevermind deals?

Jeff stared at her silently as she held his gaze and then he said, "You know, you won't get many more chances in life."

She nodded and tried to just look thoughtful. It was just a typical conversation about mortality and seizing the day. A nice sunny day with a warm breeze and children playing in front of the coffeehouse.

He continued, narrowing his eyes more with each sentence until he seemed to have his eyes closed. "I'm sure you have regrets. You should. You've done wrong things. No one does everything right. Isn't that right? Am I right? Or am I left?" When he turned his left hand over, back and forth, with each sentence, slamming the hook on his right wrist on the table for emphasis, she felt sick. "Left? Right. Right, LEFT!"

Her vision darkened around the edges. She held onto the table and stopped breathing. She struggled not to vomit and looked away from his flipping reversed hand before her eyes were drawn inexorably back. His left hand was not his left hand. His hands had obviously been removed from both wrists. His right hand had been attached to his left wrist. The thumb on his natural left hand was still intact and had been connected awkwardly to the right hand that had been attached to his left wrist. It was obviously useful for him to be able to use his hand to some degree. She'd never seen that kind of surgery. The surgeon must have been a genius to come up with that answer to an accident.

His right wrist ended in the hook, shaped like a flamingo, gloriously painted, quirky and stylish, an eccentric kind of art she normally loved. But the appendage decoration that would excite the fun, creative crowd was horrifying to her. She wanted to run away and forget he ever existed. She wanted to stomp on her nightmares and the strange wisps of false memories, to break Jeff's hands.

She screamed inside. She wanted to lock herself up away from anything so frightening forever and watch happy movies, cuddling with a fuzzy toy, and Alyssa would come over and cuddle with her and never leave and they would drink warm milk and eat cookies and sleep without dreams.

His hands seemed like a warning specific to her. As if they had been originally constructed by an evil Nevermind surgeon, to frighten her if she did something wrong. Something she regretted doing, without knowing why. Something so wrong she couldn't even remember it, because part of her had gone to her Happy Place. She knocked on the doors of that blissful state of mind, but couldn't get in.

When he flipped his reversed hand again upon the table, she felt as if his hand was in her stomach. In her vagina. In her past. In her future. She started seeing triangles, some pointed up, some pointed down. Reversed triangles superimposed on each other one up, spinning faster and faster, making a whirring sound in her mind. Her blood pressure went low and she lowered her head between her knees for a minute.

Her mind flip-flopped left to right and she felt deeply ashamed. When she raised up, he looked disappointed in her. Primal terror. *Someone else screwed up, too. Someone else has to be punished somehow. Someone in my charge. And I'm supposed to punish him.* But how could that be? It made no sense at all.

No, Jeff was just a sweet friend from social media she'd gotten together with. He happened to have a stylish hook, because he was imaginative, which was also why he wrote creative messages and felt like a kindred spirit. Bennu was a popular character, but simply ordinary, meant to entertain children. She and Jeff had different opinions about Leary, a man most people disagreed on, because Leary worked with the CIA, but at the same time was his own man who believed what he did was beneficial. That's *all* there was to it. She tried to change the topic, but he continued to ruthlessly return the conversation to Leary. She felt like shaking him to make him see the obvious. It was like talking to a ferocious boomerang.

She stared at his hook and his garbled left hand until he said, "They got blown off when I was a kid when my father gave me some bunk explosives."

"I'm sorry." She knew her mind was going in crazy directions. She'd never been paranoid, but she started to feel like she needed to get a grip on herself.

"That must have hurt a lot." She tried to figure out how his thumb was wrong, somehow. No, actually it was the only correct part about the hand. It arose from the wrist naturally. The rest of the hand - should have been on the other wrist. She gulped. She looked away politely, rather than study to see the details.

"Well, yeah. Of course it did. But Dad was a good guy. Died awhile back. I never blamed him."

"That's good of you. Does your hand hurt still?"

"I don't feel pain in it at all. It comes in handy. And look, I don't have any fingerprints. All burned off. I can get away with anything." He grinned, for the first time.

Nancy sat back. She gripped the chair.

He asked, "Do you really support yourself working in a poison company? Are you sure?" He narrowed his eyes, looking stern.

"What do you mean?"

"You don't seem like the type. What do you really do? Why don't you like the CIA? They're just a branch of government keeping us safe. What gives?" Jeff twirled his hook in the air around his ear in a gesture to indicate she was acting crazy.

"Because they covertly destroy other countries for selfish government purposes? Because they grow drugs in the countries they go to war with, and send them back here to sell and fund secret operations? They get the Nevermind to cover it all up."

"You're better than that? Where would you be if you weren't supported by the evil killer pesticides?"

Her dependence on her family connections made her blush. She grew determined to become free of her uncle and to get another job. She was going to look for a different company to work for that day.

She asked, "What are you talking about? First, they weaken the countries, not just their military, but economy too, so they can pull off the regime change. They destabilize them, impose sanctions, lower oil prices, and build bases there. The U.S. has to keep its petrodollar hegemony, right?"

He nodded, but without a sign of sarcasm.

"You know what happened after coups? Poverty. Repression. Executions. Torture. The Nevermind flips it all around in public opinion, and it gets people involved against their will. And you know those occult rituals they're rumored to have. The secret societies they're part of that sacrifice people? You're saying I'm as bad as that, because D-CIDE kills pests?"

Down deep, she agreed that there really was no difference between killing other living things and humans, except that humans were a plague upon the earth, and the survival of all the species of flora and fauna would fare better if someone did spray pesticides on everyone. If XXX in the container could be spread on the earth and only kill humans and nothing else, she'd maybe even say yes, if someone offered her the choice to save the world from extinction.

Ever since she read Rachel Carson's book that was the anathema of the pest control companies, she had kept it up on a dresser in a place of honor behind the tin box that contained Dog, next to the piano. She never opened that drawer.

She liked to go some places in her room and never others. Some drawers she didn't open, ever. Some places where she looked, her eyes refused to see; her ears would not hear. She could not tell which dreams were real and which reality was a dream, if she was honest with herself. She sometimes thought, like Ronald Reagan, that she had done things in her life that she never had. The difference was, she hadn't played a role in any movies, as far as she knew.

She tried to pretend she was a good, mature adult. Yet, her existence after the death of her father at sixteen rested on Geoff Buzner's poison money. Money from his betting on football games. She didn't look into his life. Just like when she was a little girl and sat at her desk at school and cupped her hand by her temple facing the kids at school. She'd sit in the corner chair when she could, and make it so she couldn't see any of them. In her magical system of belief, that meant they couldn't see her, either.

Jeff scooted his chair forward, bumping into the table. He held up his left hand and she became mesmerized by the haphazard scars all across the wrist where the opposite hand had been poorly stitched onto the wrist, backward. The macabre reversal triggered something visceral. She looked around quickly at the people inside the coffee shop. They were sitting just outside the corner with huge windows spreading on either side. She glanced at what each one of them had on his plate, letting her eyes circle the plates then move onto the next one. That settled her.

She felt as if the black hole inside the triangles of her imagination was darkening around the edges of her world. "I still had my thumb of this hand connected after the explosion, so the doctor took what was left of the other hand and stuck it on."

Her brain. It *wanted* to flip upside down. Roll sideways. Dyslex. Forget. Remember. Triangulate. Fly out the window. The window, the window!

"Oh, I'm sorry that happened. Can I help with anything?" Her trembling voice sounded to her as if it came from the distance, inside a well, inside another reality far away.

She couldn't believe this was happening. She felt as if she were having a nightmare in which Bennu was after her. Yet, this was a perfectly ordinary, touching moment between humans that no one else would find unusual. Jeff could speak in normal sentences in person. How thoughtless of her to react to a deformity with revulsion. She decided to order hot chocolate, hoping the magnesium in it would calm her brain so she could reason normally.

"Why do you write the way you do? It's so odd."

"It just comes to me, out of the blue." He fiddled with the flower sticking out of his pocket.

"Do you even know what it means?"

"Not usually."

"Do you ever feel like someone is putting the ideas in your head? Like, voice-to-skull technology?" She grinned and toggled her head back and forth to make him think she was joking. She was used to acting like her understanding of the documented technology the CIA was known to use, and then the Nevermind, was goofy. She was used to other people liking to feel superior by acting like that proven Intelligence program was something only weirdoes thought about.

"Ha ha. And here I was thinking I was just being poetic and profound. And typing on my phone with my hook. The phone tries to guess what I'm about to say and types out funny words. You should see how I drive." She didn't want to.

But that made total sense! He got words wrong and wrote cryptically because he was struggling with the after-effects of a terrible accident. She'd just been overreacting to auto-correct. She just needed to calm down. She breathed in the scent of the nearby flowering bushes.

They finished and he headed off. She was shaken. She jogged back home, hoping he wasn't watching to see where she lived down the block. *Ah, yes, he already knows my location.*

The early February grass was shooting up through the cracks in the uneven sidewalk. She took off her light sweatshirt as soon as she got back, as she was climbing the flight of stairs. The windows in her apartment were open and she breathed the fresh air and listened to the birds outside. They liked eating ants and the red berries that time of year. She really hoped the other tenants in the complex didn't spray the ants. She let hers overrun the place, their trails creating endlessly moving patterns across the cabinets and walls, accenting the cellar spider webs that dominated each high corner.

She walked into the living room to kick and punch. She avoided stepping on the squeaky spots scattered throughout the floor as she leapt about. After a while, she didn't care.

When she finished, she looked for a job and found one advertised at a water bottling plant in an adjacent town. She requested information. She again dug into the evangelical group her uncle was involved with. She listened to a video about it that Elias Brandon had embedded on his main page. Even with the voice distortion, his voice sounded extra deep. Fitting, if he really had gigantism. She skimmed the video until it came to Crank.

"The evangelists associated with Reverend Terry Crank consistently went to countries to do 'good work' right before those countries fell to coups that were led by certain members within the Intelligence community. They stirred up hatred against the elected leaders who were doing something bad for the U.S. economy. You know what that was? Trying to divest from petroleum, align with a country the U.S. wanted to take down for their oil.

"The Nevermind propaganda-media made the 'enemy' country look bad by talking about, ahem, 'events' that the Nevermind told them to broadcast. Check out the green screen here. The events never happened. And here, this is footage from Russia that's labeled on the news as being their local protest."

She marveled over the obvious trickery.

"In a matter of days, their new law goes into effect that will essentially pull the rug out from Western Capitalist countries' control over the world. Countries that depend on the Department of Defense, oil, bank fraud and all the rest. More countries are going independent now than we've ever seen. The people love the new regimes. But, those countries don't last long, now, do they? And we all know why that is."

The video showed scenes from coups from old black and white spy movies.

"The military evangelists are conspiring. Read the books. There's plenty of information on it, folks. It's just not on the evening news. Yet."

The video, then, showed a TV set being smashed and the pieces all contained TV anchors caught using green screen to look as if they were on location.

"Ehroh made propaganda thrillers for the Nevermind so everyone got behind the sanctions, wars, and the drone strikes. Countries trying to break free from dominance by the U.S. were taken over by factions trained by Intelligence, with puppets put into place during supposed free elections. Movies, video games, comic books, you name it, whatever the Nevermind cooked up, Ehroh offered up to the slathering public. People are buying their own stupidification and loving it. Agents are always represented as sleek, sexy, uber-efficient good guys, risking their lives to fight the bad guys in all the modes of entertainment I can think of. How about you?"

The video showed campy scenes of snappily dressed special agents, turning back and forth, holding their guns stylishly.

"The thing is, leaders all over the world are showing us better models that don't keep everyone working all day long for pennies. We could do it, too, but oil companies and bankers, Defense contractors, Big Pharma and Big Agriculture would have to put the survival of the planet over their own stranglehold on the economy. Is that going to happen? Not likely, my friends. Not likely. Maybe all we can do is just watch what's going down. And, at least, not buy toys for our kids that glorify the bullies."

Brandon's voice was masked, but she still found his tone arrogant. Still, she had to admit he was informative.

She read Jeff's post on social media he'd made shortly after leaving her. "Leary king. His servants fly in all directions and don't even need bodies to do so. Leary in sky with diamonds." He had uploaded a picture of himself picking a flower from a bush and tagged the location. It was her yard.

She looked around for the notebook where she'd been noting down his weird comments and how they related to what she'd been looking into online. The notebook was gone. She knew she had a bad memory. She needed to replace the magnesium she lost because of the stress from working a job she despised. That would help her brain recover.

She looked everywhere, and still couldn't find the notebook, and started to feel her legs weak underneath her. What if someone had broken in? Was someone trying to scare her off her search? Or keep her from remembering. No, it had to be something she did when she sleepwalked. All the things that were moved around and disappeared were just her own doing, surely.

She thought of looking next to the piano, in the drawer where she kept the childhood fan fiction stories she'd written as a child about Emily and Bennu. There were also the erotic books that had turned up in her house, slutty stuff that didn't fit her personality, so she didn't read them. She found them repulsive, yet the covers were so scintillating at the same time, images of football players, politicians, and ministers. She couldn't throw them away. She had such mixed feelings about them she never opened the drawer since she'd put them there when she first moved in long ago.

She almost opened the drawer, but couldn't make herself do it. On top of it was the Dog music box she'd had since childhood. Nancy left Dog inside the box, always: she would be embarrassed for her canine childhood friend to see the smut sitting below it in the drawer below. Keeping Dog inside the tin box, rather than springing up out of it, kept her dark subconscious impulse safe from even the canine's plastic prying eyes. She didn't have to admit to herself she must have, at one moment of weakness, bought some porn, though it was only a vague memory she didn't understand.

She lifted the cherry piano lid to see if she'd left the notebook there, and found a piece of paper torn from it under the lid. On it was a note in someone else's jagged handwriting. "Don't kill us."

Her breath came in heaves. Who could have possibly left it there, in exchange for her notebook? And why? Had Jeff sneaked in? Or Geoff?

She dropped the lid, backed away and stood by the piano, holding her stomach. She slowly danced, letting her feelings out through her fingertips, as she gathered the strength within her center. She could only go into karate practice mode to regain her sense of power, readiness for anything, for whoever was trying to get at her.

She was absolutely going to stop taking the pills that night.

CHAPTER EIGHT
The Secret Room

Emily whispered to Dog conspiratorially in the dim church hallway where they stood alone on Friday morning, as Geoff walked away from them, down the hall toward the meeting room. Leaning her full lips next to a floppy white ear, she said, "Enochian language was started by a silly man who worked for Queen Elizabeth I. His name was Mr. Edward Kelley. He and Mr. John Dee helped her take over other countries. Part of that was because of using the secret language. Aren't secrets fun, Doggiedog? Mr. Kelley was into religious glossolalia too! And then, he said he lost his memory." Emily cuddled her pet on a spring. "I'll never forget you, Dog. I'll never, never, never."

She crouched down on the hallway floor. "Hey, sweetie, since Mr. Bee left you with me this time and didn't push you back in your box, I'll show you the secret room, if you promise not to tell. It's wonderful."

She spun around, her skirt flaring out like a flower. In the darkness as she walked, she felt the wall of the hallway with her hand. She found the familiar hole, with the shape like a sigil and bent down to it. She sang into it a series of one- and two-syllable Enochian rhythms in a repeating motif of three notes.

The hidden door opened silently, and she pushed it aside, crouching down to pass through the hanging layers of crumpled gauze. Golden light illuminated it softly from behind.

She bent to light all the beeswax candles shaped like bees, with the arcane lighter hanging by the door. The candle flames swayed in the wind coming from the open window up high, farther up than she could see through. Gauze waved in front of the candles, and she bent down to move the candles farther toward safety.

She stood up and centered herself perfectly inside a square on the chessboard floor. "See, Dog - Mr. Kelley and Mr. Dee wrote the Enochian letters on squares. Just like on this chessboard. It's the angel language. You can call the angels, and they'll come! Imagine that. There are things called 'Enochian Calls' that make the angels answer." She giggled. "Isn't it amazing the codes open up doors? I think different kinds of angels live in worlds made out of notes. The doors to them have keys made out of sound. Mr. Bee was proud when he said it's new technalagaic or something like that." She hopped up and down on one leg.

Inside the miniature secret room in the church, spinning silhouettes of men and women handed each other pieces of paper with charts of letters, and sigils running through them. Each sigil represented a word in Enochian. Inside the secret room, all the spies were made of paper, hanging from the ceiling by their necks.

Emily blew on the paper spy dolls and turned to Dog conspiratorially. "Adam and Eve talked the same language before everything went bad, with the devil and all. That's what Mr. Kelley said, anyway. But to tell you the truth, I think maybe Mr. Kelley made the whole thing up! Shh, don't tell anyone! Because the language is sort of like English and sort of random. A lot of the words are ones that Mr. Kelley and

Mr. Dee used before that to talk about their spy business for the Queen. I know that because I'm smart." She stood up straight and lengthened her neck, assuming an aristocratic stance.

"But still, when people say the words, weird, weird, weird things happen. Isn't it exciting, Dog? We don't know *what* to think, do we, dear?" She snuggled it up to her and swayed back and forth, smiling.

"And now, I have to leave you here, because no one can go with me to the even secreter room. And it's time for me to go on now. But I'll come back for you, I promise. Stay!" She patted Dog's head, which bobbled around the spring, making its usual *boing boing*.

She emotionally prepared herself for what had become familiar to her, which she was never allowed to talk about to any friends. She then reached down and touched her genitals. She petted herself fervently until she had an explosion of pleasure she didn't even have a name for other than what she was told to call it: "The Special Key."

An orgasm was the only way to unlock the next level of her programmed memory code. It was required at this stage to move onto the rest of her job. Her job that she was so proud of. Her job that meant she would be paid soon in pink foil-covered chocolate bunnies and sparkly maple candy soldiers.

Once in that physiological state, she intoned the Enochian phrase to open the next special lock, which, in translation, meant: "If you tell anyone, Alyssa will die." She had no idea what an Alyssa was. She thought maybe a beautiful goddess of pie or cookies. She didn't want to do anything wrong and kill a goddess. Everything she did seemed to be about beings that were more important than people. She was more important than a regular person, they told her. She was something like the queen of the universe, but they never gave her a scepter or a crown. And what was the point of a girl being a queen without a scepter and a crown?

DARPA had created the advanced locking mechanisms that worked with sound vibrations, she was told, though she didn't know who DARPA was. She pictured a proud woman in Egyptian dress with special powers and very long hair piled high on her head.

Emily crept into the narrow passageway, settled in, fluffing her dress and sitting cross-legged on the cushions on the floor, surrounded by containers and boxes, vials, and funnels on all sides, all the way up to the low ceiling, making the space to move around in particularly tiny.

She opened a basket on the floor, took out a protective outfit covering her completely that looked something like a bee. The bee that was also seen as Ra in traditional Egyptian lore. She danced around making a buzzing sound. She put on a mask, then goggles over that, and pulled on gloves.

She opened a box, removed a container, opened it and poured its contents carefully through a funnel into a series of vials and tiny bottles. She capped some of the tiniest bottles and threaded and tied them, so they could hang as necklaces. She counted them diligently three times.

Emily lifted bottles to the light, wearing the protective gear, and poured the XXX into them, picking the proper sized funnels out of the set. Some of the bottles were flat and had long tubes coming out of them. Some had metal casings. Some were metal entirely, extremely thick, impenetrable. She filled those rectangular metal containers with the combination of the XXX and surfactant and dispersing agents.

She took down a box of Bibles and opened one up. It was hollowed out, and she put the XXX inside it; it fit perfectly. Then she intoned in Enochian to lock the clasp on the artificial Bible and then locked the box.

She took out one Bible after another, filling them, locking them, then put them all back in the box and went to another box, locking those boxes. The room seemed tiny because it was almost filled with boxes of Bibles and old cans of XXX, and their new containers of various types. She barely had room to move around.

She pulled up her mask and lifted a bottle to her nose and breathed it in. She looked around, and held it to her mouth. She opened her lips, tilted her head back, ready to pour it in.

But, she hesitated. She shook her head. "I should be a good girl and do what Mr. Bee told me. Not drink the Osiris Slain. Mr. Crank needs it. And other people need it too."

She could hardly stand not knowing what it tasted like. It was said to be special, the best concoction ever. She was supposed to never drop any or touch it. It kept the flamingo god Bennu alive. *He's borned again every time someone drinks it. Osiris Risen is very important!*

She wasn't sure what she thought about Bennu. She liked to be able to fly on his back. But, sometimes, he hurt her. Sometimes she wanted to kill him.

She wrapped each tightly closed bottle in gauze and laid them all in a metal box.

After a couple of hours of concentrated work, she smacked her lips, clapped her hands, dusting them off like she'd seen in movies. She put her hands on her hips, and said, "All done!" She closed the last box of the day and bent down to it, putting her mouth next to the hole. She sang an Enochian call with her mouth up to the malleable hole, which responded to the tones by changing shape as per the advanced technical design, locking the box so only she or Geoff's henchmen could open it.

"OK, I have to make a delivery now. A secret delivery. My favorite kind!" She put her handiwork aside as she removed her protective clothing. She went back into the outer hidden room. She heard steps outside the room and opened the door slightly, peering into the hallway. She left Dog there in the outer room when she saw her chance to walk out without being seen. She would have missed her opportunity if she'd gone over to pick up the toy.

Watching carefully for signs of people, she eased into the hallway, softly closing the door, carrying the smallest box of bottles. She jumped back into the room and closed the door behind her when she saw a shadow pass by. She hugged herself and felt like she needed to pee. She wriggled.

She couldn't wait too long, so she opened the door again. She saw no one, and so ran down softly the hallway to the bathroom. When she was done, she carried the box to the storage room for the Sunday crowd. She let herself in with the key around her neck. She approached the cages of poisonous snakes.

She reached behind them, praying out loud for protection in glossolalia, and pressed the poison box against the cloth that hung behind the cages. In the shadows, she felt the cloth brush against her hand as it yielded.

She stuck her hand into the opening and laid down the box to the spot where she was supposed to deposit it.

She drew her hand out slowly, speaking gently to the snakes to be nice and not worry; she wasn't going to hurt them.

The copperhead leaped at her, its slit eyes intense, its skin glistening smooth.

She stifled a scream as she pulled her hand away in time, as she had been trained by Bennu to have lightning-fast reflexes, just as nervous that she might drop a glass bottle of Slain as she was about being bitten. Then, she remembered

104

she no longer was holding a bottle. She'd become so used to balancing them carefully over the last hours, she had to get familiar with having her hands free again. Not having to be nervous.

The snake reared and lashed at her again. This time, as she was withdrawing her hand, the snake's mouth came within a fraction of an inch. She sobbed from fear. She shook her hand, and held it, and left the room, forgetting to turn off the light.

She was supposed to be quiet so the regular members of the church didn't know what she was doing. Only Crank and certain deacons were in the know about the game she was part of. She hoped she hadn't blown it. She had to get away fast before they found her. She had to get to Geoff to whisk her away in his car.

There was an Ehroh movie being made about someone based on her, and so, what she did had to be kept secret from everyone. No spoilers to ruin the show.

Footsteps followed her down the hallway. She walked faster. So did they. She couldn't make herself turn around to see who it was. Emily ran. All the way to Aunty Angela.

CHAPTER NINE
The Hotel

Rios had not followed his subconscious orders Angela
Ageless had given him using the Enochian code Emily had
passed along to her. His training had failed and he had not
thrown the game or carried out the precise moves at the end.
That was not OK.

The brown-skinned, handsome quarterback was meant
to become the epitome of ineptitude on the football field that
day. He'd instead won the game and garnered *more* attention
for the foreign President's withdrawal from dependence on
the U.S. dollar standard. That wouldn't do.

In her bag, Angela carried the small box she'd gotten
from Emily. She whispered goodbye to Geoff who
disappeared around the corner when she knocked on the
door at the hotel suite Monday night. She laughed
sensuously, and with a hoarse, edgy voice, called out for Rios.
"It's your angel calling," she said, her voice lower and slower.

When Rios opened the door, she reached out and tugged
on his belt. He grabbed her by the waist and pulled her to
him, pushing her against the door once he closed it, in spite
of chuckles coming from the other players in his room.
Martha had taught her well how to seduce a man to pry out
his political secrets or pass secrets to him. Because of

Martha's long and diligent training, Angela knew what to wear, how to move, how to modulate her voice. When she did a sexy little move that Martha had demonstrated for her, Angela wished she could get the image of the woman out of her mind long enough to concentrate fully on her victim.

Martha was going to have to die. Emily was a good little spyer on spies. She had caught the double-crosser passing sensitive information about her lover and Nevermind compatriot, Reverend Terry Crank.

Angela was grateful to Emily for protecting the Nevermind by turning Martha in, yet she almost wanted to spank some sense into Emily and let her know that she wasn't playing some silly game when she snitched. Emily's innocence annoyed her to no end, yet it paradoxically made her love the girl even more.

Angela and Rios felt each other's bodies fervently. He smacked her bottom and propelled her toward the center of the room. He gestured grandly toward the inevitability of the bathroom.

"I can't wait to get started," she said, with a luxurious tone.

She went into the bathroom and closed the door, taking out her diaphragm and coating it with spermicide. Before she left, she sang Enochian calls into the poison box. The childlike tune functioned as an aural key, allowing her to open it. She put the delicate miniature bottle in her diaphragm case, and dropped it in her purse, carrying it cautiously, shielding its thin glass from any dangerous surprises by holding it against her tummy.

Rios was talking to one of his buddies. She bumped him in the arm as she was focused on her dangerous seduction. "Hey, watch watchure doing!"

She took off her gloves and slapped him with them as they walked toward his bed, while his visitors dog-whistled.

They got heated under the covers as she used her special oral and manual skills with hypnotic rhythms of pleasure. Rios grinned. "Guys, you can't believe how good this is over here."

"I believe, I believe."

"So good you'll let me spend the night with you?" she asked.

"What? What are you talking about?"

"Don't you like me?" she asked, pressing herself toward him hard, and harder. With increasing speed.

"Yes! Yes, I do."

"You like me? You sure?"

"I'm sure, I like you, I like you." Eventually, the football players that were hanging out in the fancy hotel room left, other than Rios' roommate.

That night, wearing only panties and her flimsy, lacy bra, she lay listening to Rios' roommate snore. She moved Rios' arm off her chest slowly, holding her breath as long as she could. She reached to the stand and pulled out the XXX bottle. She opened it and let a drop fall into his open mouth.

She made no sound when gathering her things, holding her clothing in a wad against her chest. She put them in her bag.

She heard his breath simply stop. He had to learn his lesson about going against the greatest country in the world, even if it meant he had to go to death-school.

There would be nothing detectable in his tissues. No way to trace his death to her. No one in the room had known who she really was. She hadn't touched any surfaces without her long black gloves. If any wig hair had fallen out, well, it was just a wig. The spermicide would kill forensic evidence of DNA. She hadn't kissed him. She always sprayed her body before her encounters with a coating that kept any flakes of skin from falling, and she coated her clothes with it as well.

They never shed fibers. The Nevermind had thought of everything.

Rios should not have let himself remember about his Bennu/Enochian key training. The post-hypnotic suggestions must be obeyed. The U.S. would lose its power if Rios' President got off the dollar standard, as he was planning to do, as his last major act in his term. There wasn't much time to take down that country for the good of the U.S. Rios had been one small part of the plan for the coup. But if he had talked, he could have ruined everything.

She opened the door slightly, looking down the hall before trying to exit, scantily dressed. Hotel Security walked past and she closed the door as fast as she could without pulling it all the way and making a sound. She wasn't sure she'd pulled it far enough. Would it stick out? Would he notice a door was ajar?

His footsteps slowed, backed up. A knocking on the door. She pulled her bag closer to her as if she could hide behind it, inside it, merge with it. She hunched over. "What?" called the sleeping man.

"Your door isn't shut."

"Can't you just close it from there?" the roommate asked.

"Sure, sure." He opened the door slightly. She didn't move, hoping the darkness would hide her as his hand reached around the door knob to turn the old-fashioned locking mechanism, coming within an inch of her barely covered breasts. As he pulled his hand back, it brushed slightly against her nipple.

She waited to see what he was going to do.

He just closed the door. He must not have registered the touch of the fabric.

She waited by the door, arms and back flat against it, as the football player got up to go to the bathroom. He got back in bed without turning on the light. He turned over, sighed, and eventually his breath changed to the rhythm of sleep.

She softly sang the Enochian calls into the poison box. It locked.

And once outside the room, as the door locked, she heard Geoff around the corner saying, "All clear." She went to him and he gave her the bag. She ran to the restroom and took off her wig and trampy clothes, exchanging them for a modest long beige dress before leaving the hotel with Geoff, who drove her to Martha's house.

Martha could end up being a good discard. Throw them off Crank's trail if his girlfriend was taken down. He'd be unmistakably upset by it, so he wouldn't be perceived as a murderer.

CHAPTER TEN
Cold Turkey

Nancy went for a swim at the Y the next afternoon, enjoying the normal, non-creepy world. Tuesday was a day off for her that week, so she could relax. She was enjoying not thinking about the Agents of the Nevermind or death. Just going about life like a regular person. She ignored the obnoxious smell of chlorine and focused on the sounds of children's feet slapping the wet area around the pool. Their laughter was contagious. She had fun just wearing her overly modest one-piece swimsuit, which was covered with pictures of housewives from the 1950s smiling overly enthusiastically while ironing and cooking.

She relished the movement of her arms pushing through the water. She often dreamed about flying with that same effortless motion. In fact, her dreams the night before, in spite of her scare, had been lit up with liquid blue light, as she swam flying through the underworld, saving everything from destruction, turning it all into a shrine of itself, immobile, and perfectly colored inside the lines.

She'd done it. She'd taken no pills the night before. Only a few times in the past had she tried to get off them for only a couple of days at a time; she'd started up as soon as she noticed odd tiny blips in her sense of who she was and what she'd done in her life. She needed continuity of self and she already had so little with her fugues. What did she do during those missing times? Just sleep? Embarrassing things? Surely nothing related to the hallucinated memories she got during withdrawals. Those weren't even her own memories but about some other random people that had nothing to do with her life.

She'd face life without the pills. She'd get out from under her uncle's thumb. She was proud. She was smoking less, drinking less, eating less sugar. She was ready for whatever would happen if she just let herself feel. Just feel. She felt great.

Once she biked home, singing into the wind, she made herself wait ten minutes before getting out her laptop. It was hard. She paced. Once she opened it, she went to her favorite social media site. Jeff had just uploaded a photo of himself at a campground at a park. "Will kill off the old. Time for renewal. Reverse the story." She realized with horror that was the same park Alyssa was driving to three hours away!

No, no, no, no, no! That was just too much. She could be responsible for her friend being killed with a fucking *flamingo hook*. Her vision blurred.

She started to call Alyssa at the campground, and tell her she might be in danger of being killed. She didn't know if this was a warning to make her think about what Jeff could do or if he was really going to do it. Or if he just happened to be coincidentally camping at the same place as Alyssa. She began dialing, sweating, hitting the wrong key, dialing someone else by mistake, starting over again, clearing her throat, practicing speaking in a sane tone.

Nancy put the phone down. Really, she would tell Alyssa what? Some random nice disabled guy, who had trouble typing, was saying cryptic things, probably due to auto-correct? He must be near the park, or be hanging out somewhere there. Now, *that* would make Alyssa turn around and drive back for four hours. Right. Er, no, Alyssa would just think Nancy had lost her mind entirely.

Nancy wondered how many people would think that of her if they knew how paranoid she sounded. What if nothing Alyssa had been telling her about the world was real? No boogeymen, no Nevermind handlers, no global conspiracies, and Nancy could just relax and hang out with friends and enjoy herself. Ahh.

But seriously, what if Jeff was sent to hurt Alyssa, to warn Nancy off reporting the waste crime? Out in the middle of an empty park in the winter. "I won't look into what happened to the chemicals anymore," she said out loud to whoever might be listening in on her life. "Or mind control, the slimy Christian group or anything. I won't try to remember whatever that is from my past that's haunting me."

Then, she typed her promise, too, in case someone was logging her keystrokes. She reworded it, deleted too much by mistake, and couldn't help feeling silly about her embarrassment over her poor sentence structure. She'd never been any good at things like punctuation.

She picked up the phone and said the words into it as well, listening for bleeps and scratchy sounds of someone listening and recording. She paced, grabbing her arms. Her heart pushed up against her chest.

Alyssa was one of the most wonderful people she had ever met. Nancy's breath tried to come out through her ribs. What if her only true friend was going to die because of Nancy poking her nose into inconsequential and inevitable criminal activities? How important could it really be when the dump was full of all kinds of toxic things? It was just the dump. That's where waste went.

She practiced karate with a pretend partner who had Alyssa's dissolving face.

She couldn't sleep all Tuesday night, her heart going crazy in her body's driver's seat, speeding her body well over the limit. The timing was terrible. Wednesday she was supposed to work at D-CIDE, but she wouldn't be able to. Withdrawal symptoms were coming on strong. The chemicals from the pills were leaving her system, making her eyes gritty, her kidneys sore. Incomprehensible nightmares hinting about her reality washed across her consciousness. She was terrified of what might happen to Alyssa and tried to pray for her, though she didn't believe in God.

The horror about someone breaking into her apartment and leaving a note was overwhelming. She hummed the incomplete melody that haunted her over and over, to calm herself. She couldn't help picturing Alyssa killed by a bloody flamingo-shaped hook.

She had sometimes over the years tried to relax into self-hypnosis, to try and remember the thing that was on the tip of her memory. Just out of her reach, it taunted her ruthlessly; it gave her headaches; it gave her the feeling time was running out. Like she had been programmed to self-destruct, that there was a ticking clock, saying *Remember before it is too late, remember before it is too late*. Something about men. For someone who rarely dated, she sure had a strange feeling about men – mostly that she had something to tell them.

The image of riding Bennu through the sky into the Nevermind realms took over her mind. She rode him through the doubled triangles as each triangle turned into layers and others angled away from it, rooms upon rooms made of the geometry of sound frequencies, mathematical formulae that locked and unlocked what must remain secret.

As she lay in bed that night, she looked up at the ceiling lit up from the streetlights outside. The ceiling was a mirror, and in it, she saw a little girl reflected. She tried to remember what that meant to her. Did she have a daughter somewhere? Had she forgotten her? Sometimes she'd dreamed she had one. But no, she wouldn't be seeing her daughter in the mirror. In her delirious state, she asked, *Is that me as a child?*

She turned over, dizzy, letting her head fall over the side of the bed to bring blood to it. Beneath her, the floor was a mirror, too. She was in some sort of fun house. In the mirror, she saw another woman, sexy, worldly, nothing like Nancy at all. Who was in her room? How did that woman get in? But, when she looked up, there was no one there. When she looked down, the woman's face had turned back into hers.

When she couldn't take the emotional overwhelm anymore, the triangles began to fly. She closed her eyes. She was riding a flamingo, its beak pressed against her, dissolving into the whiteness of the clouds. It was thrilling, like riding liquid light.

When the double triangle door in her mind opened a fraction of an inch more, she flashed back to being at a church when she was young. She thought she'd never been religious. Maybe it wasn't just a phase her parents had gone through. Maybe she'd not really cared for church, so she'd blocked it out of her mind? She probably hadn't paid attention.

She remembered. The Pentecostal fervor had come over the congregation all around her. They were practicing glossolalia. And she understood exactly what a few of the deacons were saying in a special code meant just for her, amidst the sincere believers. Yet, she was not she. She was younger, but she wasn't.

Her mind felt as if it would break open when images started flooding in as the pills wore off. Was it a dream she remembered when she'd been taught a code embedded in the glossolalia long ago when she was a girl? Three deacons said the Enochian words when Crank was touring the world.

The vital importance of remembering the code exactly had been jackhammered into her brain and body. By Geoff and goddamn Jerry Crank! And . . . No, could it be? Jeff's *father*.

The father was an ugly man with a bitter, sharp mouth. Naked together in the room, under their black capes they had done something awful. If she didn't get something right that Jeff's father told her to do, she would be punished by the monster Bennu.

She couldn't believe it. If her memory was correct, she and Jeff had been forced to touch each other when they were children. She'd liked the little boy at first. He'd been gentle and she'd happily kissed him on the cheek, which was sliding and morphing into moss and mold. Her first kiss. On acid.

The pills that made me forget I knew Jeff and Crank all this time. But, did something else make me forget too? I don't think simple chemicals would be enough to keep reality at bay. She remembered Jeff hypnotically merged with a vengeful flamingo deity of powerful proportions. Osiris, the king in the Enochian game of chess, like in the Ehroh Productions classic, *Emily in Nevermind.*

The movie portrayed some rare specially chosen girls, highly trained from birth, and made into goddess queens in a globalist chess game. Some countries won, some countries lost, and some countries were sacrificed in the game the sexy, ageless girls played. Chess pieces were the closest thing the little secret agents had to dolls.

Little girls around the country dressed up like those characters in the movie for trick or treating on Halloween.

Nancy was given little white tabs of LSD on her tongue as a child and told to breathe slowly and go deep into her surreal world. Everything had melted together. *No wonder the druggie Nevermind's hypnosis techniques are legendary. They're brilliant. Hats off. Some other girls live in the Nevermind too, don't they? Terrified of Bennu chasing them down when they do something wrong. His feathers flapping, his beak scooping, his screech taking over their world.*

Jeff became intertwined with her uncle Geoff. His right hook man. His extension that did his bidding. She remembered only Bennu in her dreams. When she remembered her uncle doing something bad to her, the image of Bennu diverted her and terrified her. Flying. Flying, flying to the beautiful clouds. A god to love. A god to fear.

Nancy thought about movies she'd heard of but never seen: *Manchurian Candidate* and *Bourne Identity.* Was that kind of deliberate personality splitting, for the sake of Intelligence and political intrigue, actually real? She contemplated Patty Hearst and Sirhan Sirhan.

She looked online. Brandon had a video. Of course. He'd infiltrated a Nevermind ritual that bonded the members for life and made them eternally loyal to their oaths. The members went through symbolic rituals to become Osiris Slain. Their personalities were torn apart and remade in another image more useful for the Agency, becoming Osiris Risen.

Fortunately, some members were allowed to leave the organization when they became disillusioned. Some of the Nevermind's corruption had been publicly exposed during the time of the Human-Growth Hormone giants, in the early 1990s, when the giant U.S. President had instigated the Occult Revival. That discovery liberated some of the members, including Helen, the author of Alyssa's book.

The more the public learned about the Nevermind, the more fragile became their position in the underground war with anti-propaganda journalists like Brandon. And he was impossible to prosecute, because he had secrets that would take down the whole organization. If anything happened to him, the information was set to release.

In her hallucinations, Bennu was the arrogant ruler who set her up high as being queen-like and full of power and then pulled her down onto him, skewering her with humiliation as he morphed into a flamingo, mocking her, making her question what she was seeing, unable to tell anyone from a fear of sounding insane.

She felt sorry for Jeff. He'd been trained in the occult tradition all his life, the same way she had. They'd made love tenderly as children, and she'd learned to help him accept the deformity of his hook and reversed hand, kissing them. They'd both cowered under his father and her uncle's gaze. The children had held to each other for comfort before she was made to forget him as a real person entirely.

How strange Jeff must have felt when that happened. Did he miss her love? He must have felt awful that she didn't remember him at all. Her look of revulsion at the coffee shop must have been easy for him to read.

Past and current realities combined into one. She was the same age she was then. Like she'd never aged. Like some of the memories were really her as a child, decades before, and some were her as a child last week. In her vivid memory, the oldest Pentecostal deacon in the church, even his Adam's apple sagging from age, yelled out in the fake glossolalia code.

She was able to decode the glossolalia: it was about the football game Rios was supposed to throw. That thought made Nancy feel very strange. She was turning into more than one person at once. The deacon's Enochian sentences described mathematical configurations. The rest of the congregation had no idea. How did she know that? And what did any of those memories have to do with her real life?

The football player was supposed to protect the Anglicized empire somehow from his own country's progressive freedom. The childish song she'd written so long ago had something to do with everything she was discovering, too. She just couldn't figure out what. It was all coming back to her, as if she were walking a labyrinth with psychedelic images projected onto dense fog. And there were only funhouse mirrors for the sky and ground.

She remembered being in church recently. Three deacons who were not in an ecstatic trance like the others in the church had been looking over at her, searching her face. At that moment, they were probably betting big money for the team to lose, as planned. And, with some of that money, Martha was no doubt going to buy that sparkly Cadillac she'd been going on about.

How could Nancy prove all this existed? And who would she prove it to? It was government policy to do dubious things in the name of national security. Without things like betting on the games she helped throw, how would the Nevermind fund its black ops?

How do you report memories that are all tangled up and impossible to place in your past? How do you turn in a criminal when the criminal is you? And when outing an Agent is a crime?

She panted, going in and out of consciousness and degrees of awareness as the drug left her body, built up toxicity until she drank more water, and it pushed her over the edge. She dreamed, but wasn't sure if she was asleep or awake. She had a vision of someone delivering "her" to Rios' room. When, she couldn't say. But no, it wasn't her. It was a slutty, dangerous friend of hers. Still she didn't remember meeting the friend or hanging out with her.

And how many others like Rios had there been that her slutty friend had sex with? Why would Nancy be friends with such a tramp? Geoff, Jeff, and Bennu: their superimposed images flipped over and over in her mind, upside down as a flamingo, right side up as her leering uncle, then superimposed, both of them at once, flashing, spinning. She clenched her teeth and tightened her abdominal muscles, struggling to keep from being pulled through the spin into the land of Nevermind.

The slut had tried to keep her good side to the camera when she recorded her unspeakable sexual experiences with Rios in the bed. And why had Rios been in a trance? And how had she spoken to him in a language she didn't understand? How did she know how to program someone's subconscious like that? And how did Nancy know what the slut thought?

While having sex with him, she'd worried about how she'd gained weight, and how that would look, if it became important for the tape of their acts to be released to public. She knew all her messages to Rios were not supposed to be written down, nothing said louder than an intimate, indecipherable whisper. Blackmail-worthy perversions. Acts that could keep Rios doing exactly what the Nevermind wanted him to do for the rest of his life.

Why was she thinking of it as herself doing these things? Was that what she did when she blacked out and went on her fugues? She wasn't sleepwalking?

She needed to read that lost book that she'd stolen from Alyssa. That wasn't the only book about entertainers, religious figures, and politicians being handlers making the rounds of conspiracy scuttlebutt.

Was her mind playing a trick on her because she'd heard a little about them? Was this like all those people who started remembering alien abductions after seeing science fiction movies, just like that? She hoped so. If she could debunk her memories, she could let it all go, once and for all.

The woman who wrote the book, Helen, reminded her of one of the sisters she remembered flying out the window with, turning colors as they crossed the threshold, led by Bennu, who flew underneath them in the air and they rode on him.

It seemed to her they'd been forced to watch the Nevermind's Ehroh movies together and go in and out of the characters in waves. Was that just conspiracy theory sinking into her subconscious? They had been trained during traumatic nights on drugs and hypnosis, pain and pleasure, and the horror of the hands. The hands. The girl could fly into the other space when Jeff was traumatizing her. He became her warning. The omnipotent Bennu.

The girls would live in the worlds of the movies while they were being tormented, would become the characters to escape the trauma, and fantasize they had their super-human abilities. Nancy got it: even more effective movie-based programming would happen across the country when *Return to Emily: The Reversal* came out. Were they Nevermind Agents working for the U.S. petrodollar hegemony?

The U.S. populace would agree with all the coups the U.S. fomented in other countries, because the Nevermind's propaganda always worked. The newscasters, the movies, video games, music, Halloween costumes and everything else Ehroh created for the Nevermind would illustrate the international dynamics in ways that made hatred of competing leaders appealingly patriotic. Strong emotion, based on narratives created by the lies on the nightly news, made the reality of foreign policy easy to ignore.

Minute by minute, the drugs left her body, taking with them the particularly ironic delusion that she was, well, *deluded.* In her increasing sanity, she realized what she'd been calling illusions were real memories. Horrible ones.

She knew she'd remembered something earlier, but she didn't know what. New bits of memory took precedence over old revelations, which faded out. She could hardly stand the horror. She felt as if she was being torn apart by a flamingo's beak, broken into pieces that flew into the blue of the sky and disappeared into it, as the sky itself became invisible and far away, far, far away.

Each piece of her psyche that went flying could have its use to the U.S. Each had its specialties. All of them funding the Nevermind and making the Agency maintain the power of the country, keeping it on an even keel. Everyone knew the Nevermind's underground activities were what made their lives continue on comfortably. People just looked the other way and didn't think about it.

If the other countries weren't taken down when they threatened the supremacy of the petro-dollar, the lifestyle that people had grown accustomed to would shatter. But, people didn't want to face living in the U.S. without its insider trading and monetary value adjustments, assassinations, drug and arms money laundering, coups, and right wing evangelists in the military bringing in political votes with threats of burning in hell. If citizens rose up en masse to defend the countries trying to gain economic independence, destabilization of power would hit the U.S. like a sledgehammer.

She mused over how, when the CIA was admonished for its crimes, the National Endowment for Democracy took over many of its most unsavory functions. The politically savvy part of herself was polishing her mind as the hours went by in her room, as she sweated and let the rain fly in her windows. She couldn't get up and close them. State secrets and historical policy entangled with her nausea and shivers.

She thought about how the Nevermind's Occult Revival had been established when *Giant Jack* comics were all the rage, and Ehroh created such compelling Theosophical propaganda movies, games, and news reports the whole world was entranced.

She went into spasms when she reviewed how some Dominionist evangelists, including Crank, had been instrumental in the country's longstanding policy of using U.S. Intelligence provocateurs to foment coups. The military stole drugs and oil, money and art from the countries they took down. The drugs funded the black operations that needed to stay off the records. It was best for some in Congress not to know. Working with the Council of Foreign Relations, the Nevermind made that easy. It made it easy for everyone not to know anything. And *Return to Emily: The Reversal* looked like it would glorify it in a sickening way.

Alyssa had told her about Luis Angel Castillo, who had been programmed with multiple personalities, one of which was meant to assassinate President Marcos. Castillo was even tied in with JFK's assassination. MKULTRA had been functioning at Bordertown Reformatory when he was there. And DeFreeze, Patty Hearst's brainwasher, was there too when the SLA was being created, and he was being changed into what the CIA needed him to be. He was brainwashed at Vacaville Medical Facility himself.

Alyssa had looked at her with a searching look when telling her about Candy Jones. Nancy was starting to understand why her buddy might have had questions about how her behavioral patterns coincided with that poor woman's supposed multiple personality that she claimed was created to make her become a perfect courier for the CIA.

What was worse, she felt there was a serious deadline she was supposed to be paying attention to. Something Crank had said in church about getting the last of the donations from the members for a delivery of Bibles overseas.

As the chemical potency lessened in her body, she remembered fleeting scenes of renditions and prying government secrets and relaying the information about world leaders to the Agency. She remembered bits of dinners with investors and passing carefully guarded hints about black ops that would be affecting the stock market. Insider trading and fixing sports games were easy. Killing was harder.

Her sharpest moment of clarity came to her in a terrible flash. Rios had won the game, against her hypnotic orders. She grew so cold nothing could warm her. She breathed on her hands and rubbed them together, put them in her pockets. Her breath came faster. She was in trouble. Terrible trouble, unless she could make herself valuable to the Agency. They wouldn't kill her if she could do a good save.

They'd kill Alyssa, if Nancy couldn't stop it. Geoff had promised her that. He'd send Jeff, his goon, to do the dirty work.

Geoff, certain corrupt deacons, and their cronies in the Agency expected to win big from betting big bucks on the fixed football game. They were expected to turn over most of the winnings to the Agency. That funding made it easier for the Nevermind Agents to continue taking down countries with a combination of Charismatic evangelists and politics, drug running, and assassins, putting their own petro-puppets into place.

The halftime show had persuaded the public to believe in mystical fairy tales rather than look at facts. To believe in illogic. Not only that, the show was a message to sleeper spies.

This was not the kind of thing one reports to the police. It was U.S. foreign policy in action, typical of Intelligence ploys for decades. Some of it sanctioned, some of it symbolic occult ritual enacted by the Nevermind in the ways people had come to embrace through Ehroh movies.

The halftime show was a declaration of dark sacrifice. And one death was to be Rios' if he didn't go along with the program planted in his mind. The Nevermind loved to play out the sacrifices in deadly ritual during Rosicrucian Enochian Chess games. Ritual that made its way into Ehroh movies. The sacrifices always got cleaned up in mass media. Only internet rumors would touch the topic. Elaborate analysis of the meaning of each moment of the sinister theater revealed the motives.

But what could people do who saw and understood the rituals? Simply humor their friends who weren't in the know, smile at their community barbecues and agree that the Super Bowl had been a killer time.

No *wonder* she sometimes came to from her fugues while playing her piano, not remembering how she got there, where she had been before. It wasn't simple sleepwalking or amnesiac fugues. No wonder Geoff supplied her with the pills that kept her from remembering these things. She'd never let herself question her uncle's generosity when he handed her the bottles. She'd just taken them because they made her feel good. Sometimes even invincible.

She wore a compartment ring and a compartment necklace. A compartment earring had a pouch sewed into her underwear. All of these had some of the tiny pills in them in case she got stranded somewhere. She'd hidden her pill habit from Alyssa and everyone she knew. Her addiction had been her darkness. Now she realized just how big a shadow it had cast on the light of her real light.

She threw up the past onto the floor of the present. She never wanted to eat again. She ran to the bathroom to throw up some more and wipe her face, rinse the nastiness from strands of her hair, drink water from the tap.

Crying, she went into her living room to dance, with minimal movements and shaky legs. She ignored the smell of vomit and pretended she was listening to Schoenberg piano music and was supposed to be out of sync. She told herself everything she thought she was remembering was all sick, vile imagination. She shouldn't read popular sensationalized stories about mind control. How many other perfectly ordinary people had read them and then suddenly thought it happened to them too?

She'd believed so many things as a toddler. Like the Tooth Fairy. God. She made up stories about having wings and being an angel when she was a child. She'd thought at times she remembered spirit guides and aliens, past lives, gnomes. She'd see the giants who had taken Human Growth Hormone when they were teens and acquired gigantism and she'd still get fluttery as if she had something magical about them, something superior to an ordinary human. Obviously, she had an overactive imagination.

She felt the red spot on her throat. Still there. She wanted it to stop itching. More than anything else, she wanted to forget what she had remembered.

She blew her nose, cleaned up the vomit, put on some makeup, and biked to the corner store for some wine and cigarettes.

She felt silly buying wine first thing in the morning on a day she was supposed to be working, but she told herself it was for a good cause.

"Hello, my friend," said the dark man behind the counter. He was always so nice to her. No one in her neighborhood ever looked at her funny.

She didn't like how red wine made her tongue and teeth purple and stained her teeth. Wouldn't look good to Julio. Not that he was there. She just pictured him with her all the time, an invisible partner, the person who made life worth living, the person she most looked forward to seeing. Well, and Alyssa. But that was part of what she was trying to forget. The danger her friend was in. No, she *wasn't*. She was just fucking camping. It would all be fine. Drinking wine was supposed to be healthy. Antioxidants. She should get organic next time.

Nancy wanted to live a long, happy life. She wanted to be good to herself. She never had lived out her ideal of a harmonious, non-toxic life. She'd eaten junk food grown in terrible conditions that were doing awful things to the planet. She'd stuffed her feelings with the sensations the addictive foods gave her instead.

She saw something out of the corner of her eye: someone jumping behind the corner of the building. It was not a very safe area in general, by the liquor store, on the edge of the lowest rent district. That made it feel even creepier. She biked home from the liquor store fast.

The exercise cleared her head. She sang and everything was a little better. She was just a little crazy. It was OK for sexy girls to be crazy. It was almost considered a plus.

She watched Brandon videos and searched the internet for anyone saying the giant had behaved wrongly. She found plenty of trolls, but that was it. She wanted to trust him as much as Alyssa did. She wanted to contact him. But, that wouldn't look good if anyone caught her at it. And if she just told him what she remembered, that would do nothing. If it was real, it would be classified anyway and taken away. If it wasn't real, it could be used against her by psychiatrists if they ever decided she was nuts.

She needed to create some kind of public scene that couldn't be unseen. Something people would be fascinated by and for which they would look for an explanation.

Tantra Bensko

Her memories came in waves and then went away, and she was left, moment by moment, uncertain what any of it had meant, if anything, and then it was gone. She tried writing them down, but they made no sense. Just fragments, words she couldn't read, mysterious diagrams, and a few sentences that she didn't even remember writing and had no context for.

She told herself she would *not* take the pills. She reveled in her sweaty resolution to continue her detox. Her skin itched and she felt as if spiders were crawling on it. She thought she saw a giant spider on her elbow, and brushed it off, but felt nothing. The very air around her itched. Her body felt as if it were floating outside her skin.

Days passed. She called in sick for an indefinite time. She'd never be able to keep her job at D-CIDE. She would never be able to get another one. She'd be penniless.

But wait. Her memory told her that her real job was with the Nevermind. Didn't they ever *pay* her? She should have been paid so much more money it made her blood boil. But, they couldn't. Nancy would have no way of knowing where the money came from. And, they had to keep her in the dark about having anything to do with the Agency.

She fantasized that if, it was true, she'd take the whole bottle and commit suicide. She *deserved* to die if she had done those crimes in the name of U.S. Intelligence. The Nevermind was a brutal, manipulative, unscrupulous organization and she wanted nothing more to do with it. It kept the Defense Industry manufacturers wealthy with one war after another, and all the secret agent movies glorified them. But would they let her walk away?

Her stomach cramped and her head pounded. She drank all the water she could, but getting up to refill water bottles was almost impossible. She didn't make it to the bathroom once, then twice, then so many times she couldn't count. Her bed became a mess, like a person turned inside out, filled with vomit, feces, urine, and finally, blood in the mucous she coughed up from her lungs.

She curled up in bed and pulled the wet stinking covers over her head. She grabbed her childhood toy, the box that contained Dog inside it. She pressed its hard edges against her skin until she cried out. Were the weird symptoms from a physical addiction, or emotional? She couldn't tell. *Reality* seemed to be the main effect of stopping the pills. And she wasn't ready. The memories and the insider understanding of the life of a spy, forced to tread the realm of the Nevermind, was just too much.

No *wonder* her body didn't show her age. It was a fact that alters had different physiologies, like lower inflammation, blood pressure, blood sugar, hormone levels and all. She, at least, had been immersed in the fountain of youth.

Splitting was an adaptive mechanism forced on her by the Bee of Ra cult. Her psyche was a survivor. It knew how to handle her life. She petted her body, thanking it for finding a way to compartmentalize the trauma. She made herself breathe more deeply. She thought about what her piano teacher had told her. There was a way to become more authentic. She could do it. She could. Withdrawal was only part of it.

She remembered being taken as a toddler on trips with the pest control operator when her father thought she was at school. He'd pushed her down onto the animals he killed with the poison. He'd threatened to use it on her. To scare her, he'd locked her up in the cellars of houses while he worked. He'd arranged bones in patterns and told her she had to figure out what the shapes they made meant or he would kill her. He'd held her down until she imagined being like the sexy lady doll she was given each time the torment was over. Until she performed sexually for the pest control operator, who was an Agent. And then, for the diplomats, judges and bankers. When the D-CIDE serviceman had died from chlordane poisoning, she had not shed a tear.

The phone rang. When she answered, there was someone urgently speaking Enochian. Then, the sound of a clock ticking loudly. A tone and a whir. The man hung up.

She was transformed by the inner message the man left. A triangle fluttered behind her eyelids. It was nearly time for what she must do. She had to prepare for her job her country relied on. She had no choice. She had to take a pill.

Her skin was clammy with beads of sweat. Her breath got so bad she pulled the wet covers down to breathe fresh air. How did people handle truth? She'd barely glimpsed it, and she knew it was some horrendous monster bigger than she was. *She* was bigger than she was.

She lunged across the room, crawling toward the bottle she'd put in the bottom of her closet under clothes.

She took a Jolly West. She'd made it without any pills at all from Tuesday through most of Friday. She would have to say goodbye to everything she'd remembered. She didn't know how memories would come back to her again or if any ever would. Every time before, when she'd started the Jollys again, she remembered almost nothing from her time without them. But back then, she wasn't trying to remember, to become her authentic self, to play the song from youth. She had to be only her front alter if she was to obey the command. The command, the command. She burned the notes.

She covered her head and rocked, her vertebrae making a sound against the hardwood floor over and over. When she felt well enough, she opened her rolltop desk and rummaged around, her hands shakier than normal because of her Acquired Porphyria, finding a mini-chocolate bar in the back. She hugged herself and rocked as she ate it.

She drooled on her shirt, staining it with chocolate, but she didn't care. Mucous and saliva dribbled down her chin and dried, as the fan was pointed at her, making it feel crunchy. She licked it, and grimaced, disgusted with herself. Why couldn't she be dainty like other women? She didn't even feel like getting out the corkscrew to open the wine bottle. She looked for it all through the drawer but couldn't find it.

She used a knife to try to open it and threw it on the floor.

The bottle's top smashed. She poured some into a mug, picking out the pieces of shattered glass. She filtered the remaining tiny pieces with her front teeth. She couldn't function yet with that degree of understanding. For her to stand it, her life had to come back slowly, bit by bit. First, she had to forget most of what she had just remembered. She had to drip reality, opening the clamp on her IV just a little bit. And then, flushing out the truth fast, if it became too dense in the blood.

She curled up in a ball, holding herself against the cold rain running across the floor from the open window and closed her eyes into dark.

CHAPTER ELEVEN
Presidential Suite

Angela knew it was her turn to show the visiting President her exotic body that Saturday night. She opened her bra, to show the extraordinarily upturned wonders inside. She knew the diminutive, brown-skinned President would pick her from the bunch. The others had been chosen to be less beautiful than she was, to make his Saturday night entertainment decision easy.

The graceful President walked toward her and took her hand gallantly. His black eyes and long lashes were artistic and his cheekbones high. She didn't want to have to pry secrets from him while pretending to be kind. In fact, that was the last thing in the world she wanted. Some part of her loved him. If only the U.S. was run like his country, she wouldn't have to do the underhanded things she did. Honesty and integrity would prevail. Nancy could have been left alone if she'd grown up there instead of being split into compartments by the Agents of the Nevermind.

Angela was relieved Nancy had taken a pill the night before and again that evening, especially because, so recently, Angela and Emily had been on the brink of extinction from the loss of the chemical in Nancy's bloodstream. If Nancy went too long without the full dosage of pills, Angela's persona and Emily's persona would first come forward, and Nancy would gain some elusive and ever-disappearing insights. But then, the alters would die off. Nancy wouldn't ever be able to remember anything about them again. Nothing would ever make sense to her again.

Angela wasn't made in a way that would allow her to revolt. But, her closer connection to Nancy during the detox days made her waver in her determination to work for the financial benefit of the elite. She wanted to retire early and let the pieces of foreign intrigue fall where they may. But, she didn't want to die and leave Nancy a mere shell. If Angela and Emily died, Nancy would have only a small part of her critical faculties left. It would have the effect of gory brain damage.

She would most likely give in to her genocidal fantasy of pouring XXX in the water bottling plant to reduce the population a bit and give nature a better chance. She could begin with poisoning everyone closest to her, like Julio and Alyssa.

Angela wanted to relax the muscles in her arms to soften into the President's when he held her. They walked arm in arm across the Presidential suite at the best hotel in her city. She wanted to spend days with him, not just hours, to talk with him about foreign policy and how he felt about the United States, and what other places he might explore that were great fun.

After her better glimpse into Nancy's innocent morality without such a strong wall between them, she was starting to care more deeply for the President, her prey. She wanted to just go someplace with him and laugh and sing and dance. To be treated like she mattered as a whole person, not just a body. She could tell he liked that kind of thing better anyway. She saw it in his eyes.

She'd never had the chance to just enjoy herself. She only saw people innocently dating and making love for love on TV. She wished she could be the playful magical moonchild that Emily was.

She longed for it more than ever. *Please, please, Nancy,* she willed. *Remember the rest of the song you wrote when you were a girl and take us into yourself before we have to self-destruct. Let us do the things we want to do. Love. Grow up. Everything. You just have to escape from Geoff and Crank and find some safe hideout.*

She adjusted the tiny recording device she wore as an earring as she played with her hair flirtatiously. The other women were given cocktails in a distant part of the suite, and their voices could overpower what the President said. So, she cupped her hand over her ear when he talked at first, claiming to be slightly hard of hearing. "Too much partying to loud music," she told him. "I know how to party. I like to do it to it!"

The President's mouth wavered. She realized that was a new phrase for him. She wanted to comfort him by explaining it, but decided that could make him feel condescended to, so she swayed her hips instead, as she said it again, with more emphasis. "Do it *to* it, baby!"

He grinned widely, his white teeth flashing, and said, "Yes, indeed."

His bodyguard, standing watching her and all the other women, smiled too, and she shot him a seductive look so he didn't feel left out. "I'm glad you picked me," Angela said. "The other women were trying to get me to have sex with them. And you know what the Lord says about homosexuality. It's never OK." She said this in a tone that could make it possible to bond with her if he was officially pretending to agree with the Dominionists in the U.S. Military.

They were aggressively evangelizing the area and agitating people against "sins" like homosexuality. They were training with the Nevermind strategists and case officers at the U.S. Embassy, spearheading what was meant to look like a spontaneously arising religious right wing movement of the people.

She also said her statement with a tone that could suggest she was exaggerating and making fun of the religious aversion to homosexuality. The statement was actually ready to provide an outlet for him, if he wanted to relax with her in such a private setting. "Homosexuality is weakening every country that's tolerant of it. I hope you keep yours strict." She watched his face as she breathed the words in an obviously overdone sultry voice while she took off her top and looked back over her shoulder at the women at the bar.

He got it. He laughed and squeezed her hand. She was in.

"Of course, if it's something you like, sweetheart, we can always arrange that." She cupped her hand to capture his response. She couldn't read his look so she whispered, "I've heard it's only really *baaad* if it's between men. When you think of the word, you think of men, right? Not women. Sometimes, if a man only watches lots of women have sex, it's not considered being homosexual, now is it? At least, not in our country. Is it in yours?"

"Well, watching you enjoy other women does sound intriguing to me. And it couldn't possibly make me gay, could it?"

She was under orders to take him down fast. The Pentecostal evangelists, led by Crank, were setting his populace on fire, backing a pro-U.S. fascist drug lord leader trained by the Agents of the Nevermind. The petrodollar kept the U.S. imperial wars going. The demand had to stay high. There had to be a coup before his scheduled switch away from the dollar standard.

Angela nodded to the women. They came over two by two, holding each other, kissing passionately as they approached, as if they were doing it of their own accord after drinking perhaps one too many cocktails.

"Oh, those rascals," said Angela. The women, all of them, showed their enjoyment of the moment, some of them moaning, one even purring. One brushed up against him and another reached out and caressed his hair briefly. "Should I send them away? It looks like they can't contain their interest in you. I can understand why."

She pulled out her pocket litter — "for a good time call" cards, a sexy horoscope mini-scroll, and strawberry condoms — and placed them on the table.

"I thought it was interest in each other."

"Nothing turns women on like someone like you. It makes us hot. You understand." Martha had taught her his profile. That woman had thoroughly researched what made him cave.

"I think I do, yes." He stood as if entranced by the women.

Angela led him to a red velvet daybed beneath a bay window framed in gold. One of the women handed her a cocktail. Angela drank a sip and kissed the President, transferring the drink to his mouth as she pressed her breasts up against his chest.

Some of the swallows stood next to them and removed articles of clothing slowly, touching each other as he watched. One of them sat down on the daybed with the President and Angela, leaning in against them. Angela pulled his face to her and kissed him while one of the women took off his shirt.

If only he could have seen the light and given precedence to the U.S. like a good boy should. She was enjoying her legend as a simple seductress. But, he had been naughty. Oh, so naughty. She spanked him and he grabbed her and moaned, his eyes closing. He had underestimated the power of the country that ruled the world, as it should, and he would have to pay. Everyone always had to pay. Stealing someone else's hard-won power was not OK.

Meanwhile, while all his attention was on Angela, as he kissed her with his eyes closed, the flat-chested woman who was leaning against him and moving her body against his slipped off her dress.

The woman who had handed Angela the cocktail stood in the perfect position to record it on video with a tiny camera. She spun around to show other women getting intimate with each other next to him.

Her honey trap would rile up his citizens against homosexual acts. Once people saw the video, they'd feel betrayed by him. They'd be ready to fall for the U.S. coup within the required number of days.

He would never be able to trace Angela for retribution, because she didn't technically exist. She was nothing like Nancy, particularly wearing that dark wig, covered in fake tattoos and a very dark spray-on tan, with fake fingernails and lashes.

The woman on the bed with them took off her panties, and it was clear that she was actually a man: a raven. The raven unbuttoned the President's pants and went down on him as he buried his head in Angela's breasts.

As soon as enough video was taken to erode the President's career, the man put his clothes back on and left the room without the President noticing. A different woman sat down and engaged the couple sensuously, and a night of true debauchery began. Patriotism was sometimes pleasure.

Tantra Bensko

Sometimes, so much Angela could hardly stand the intensity of her orgasms as her cries echoed through the mirrored room.

CHAPTER TWELVE
Chess

Emily's body lay unmoving on the bed, Sunday morning, in a room one floor below the Presidential Suite of the hotel. Her eyes stared without blinking, as Geoff put on her a frilly, flouncy dress and black and white checkerboard tights. He stuck a box in her hands and when he opened the lid a doppelganger of Dog, this one dirty, with a shredded ear, popped out. Her expression changed. Her voice high and cute, though tired, she said, "Oh, hello!" She looked around startled, getting her bearings. She gave Geoff a big hug and petted his face with Dog II's fuzzy head.

Geoff asked her in an exaggeratedly excited voice if she'd like a petit-four. She shaded her eyes from the studio lights and wiped the sweat from her forehead.

She clapped her hands and exclaimed, "Yes!" Her eyelids were droopy and her head hurt. As she held the treat to her mouth with one hand, he held her other hand, walking with her down the hall to a meeting room, exactly beneath the President's suite.

Its placard announced, "John Dee Room." Geoff pulled up his chair opposite Crank's, facing a large rectangular table with black and white squares. The other chairs were already filled with men in purple suits and a woman in a red silk dress showing extreme cleavage. The drapes were black, matching the floor's large black and white squares.

The centerpiece on the table was a skull, with a ruby in one of its front teeth. On top of the skull, a fuchsia cone pointed toward the center of the ceiling. Four men, standing around the edges of the table, chanted Enochian as they stared at it, all of them wearing extremely tall matching conical hats as well. They wore black heavy wool capes, accenting the paleness of their thin faces.

"Father, send your charms up to the President above," said Crank to the skull, with a ceremonial grandeur.

Emily held her finger with the ring up to the ruby on the tooth. Emily went inside the color, into a room that seemed to be almost made of frozen liquid red light.

The director, who had been coaching the man shooting video, took notes. He glanced at the youngest man, who looked querulous. "This will make a good mock-up for the main scene in *Return to Emily*. It will be the signature even in the shortest trailer. We'll train a new generation of excellent split-agents with this movie."

The man holding the boom said, "An image of this scene in animation will be on the poster."

A man sitting on a throne in the corner, his face lit with red light that cast deep shadows, narrated for the camera: "Enochian chess represents the conflict within humanity's dual nature made up of rationalization for our methods of fighting for our survival. With Rosicrucian and Freemasonic chess however, it's more complex, as the self is divided."

One of the men around the table said, "Begin," and banged a small gong. A mage addressed his patter to invisible archangels for fifteen minutes in Enochian. The players put their hands on the Enochian chess board stocked with pieces representing Osiris, Isis, Horus and all the rest.

Beneath the table, the other female chess player played footsie with Emily, moving her foot along Emily's leg to her knee, then resting it there. Emily reached down and held the foot on her knee and distractedly caressed the high heeled shoe in rhythm as she played silently, her eyes wide.

She felt luxuriously different from usual. She wondered why. She felt herself waft in and out of feeling like herself and awareness of someone else, someone she once was and would become, and other people in her life she thought she knew somehow as if she'd met them in a dream and they were solidifying around the edges of her consciousness. Alyssa. A woman named Alyssa. She wanted to get to know her. She wanted real friends. Any friends.

The game's die indicated she should take on the Red role, as her pretty ally became Yellow. They strove to capture the kings of the other two players. Her ally's dress smelled fine. Emily breathed in deeply, bending toward her kitty-cornered across the table. The woman seemed awfully serious to her. Emily reached out and tried to tickle her, but the woman only told her to stop. Alyssa would never shush her, Emily thought. Whoever Alyssa was.

The cameras were on her, and she shyly avoided looking into them. She watched herself in the mirrored wall as the lights made sweat drop down her forehead. The angle of the bulbs made her irises look like they went back forever, filled with emerald green miracles.

Her ally would be leaving soon. Emily played the game slowly to make the woman be there with her in the room longer. Their opponents came on like a tornado as she stared at the skull of Father, looking in the eye sockets from which incense smoke emerged.

Next to it, a bottle of mezcal caught the light, creating a rich copper tone. At the bottom of the bottle was a worm and on the label was an image of Emily holding a rope that led to Bennu the flamingo. She was holding Dog, and behind her were skulls and worms. "Glossolalia" was the name of the Mezcal. The members in the room passed the bottle around. Emily drank too. The movie crew was not included in the passing of the intoxicating sacrament.

"Are ya working hard or Babylon working?" Emily asked Reverend Terry Crank. He laughed uproariously at her joke. She always liked laughter.

When Emily came out of her mathematical trance of labyrinthine red memory, she realized she and her ally had won. The others solemnly repeated Enochian language in four-part harmony and then finished with "All hail Osiris Slain unto Osiris Risen. The transformation is complete. The Bee of Ra is placated. The dollar prevails."

It was time for the divination. They each rolled the six-sided die to determine the order in which they would take turns to ask their questions. They set the Ptah piece in the center, and then, all went after capturing it with their Kings, electrifying the ritual intent each querent kept in mind.

"Now it's time to contemplate the relation of your pieces to the squares and determine your messages from the divine."

They all closed their eyes and sat in silence. After a while, the gong rang, and they stirred.

The cameraman, light and boom operators started packing up their equipment, congratulating Emily and her ally on the ritual that would reverberate throughout the Agency and lead to vast changes in the balance of power.

CHAPTER THIRTEEN
Piano

Nancy wasn't sure she was up for company. She'd been through a lot that week — more than she even knew, during her blackout. Obviously, she'd gotten into mischief. Even though she'd been home feeling nauseous and headachy Tuesday through Friday, she couldn't remember what happened during that time. Time was going fast.

But still, there was the sense that something might come together, that she could access youthful spontaneity and sensuality and have more fun with her life than she'd expected. She couldn't wait to show her piano teacher how that openness translated into music. She was nervous it wouldn't be enough to make up for how little she'd practiced. Would he drop her as a student since she hadn't learned the hardest exercise?

She took three-quarters of a pill.

The Sunday evening lesson was beautiful. She served ginger tea and put out her favorite tiny orange bowls and poured almonds mixed with macadamia nuts into them. She wore yellow striped tights and espadrilles. She stood in front of the curtainless open windows in the living room. A young man wearing a top hat and filmy scarf passed by the street.

She got excited by his fashion sense and leaned out the window. He waved. *He probably thinks I'm as young as he is. I'm so lucky never showing my age.* She stood back from the window and lifted one knee, looping one arm underneath it and with that hand and the other at the same time, she waved at him.

He broke out laughing and stopped, lifting his knee and looping an arm underneath it, waving back, almost falling over as he hopped around to balance. She heard people walking past on the sidewalk commenting on how much they loved Chopin. She warmed when she heard on the street below a delicate and sedate voice of a lady complimenting her to her friend walking with her: "We're so lucky to have someone living in the neighborhood who can play free concerts for us like that, aren't we?"

When the teacher arrived, his gray mustache was twirled up on the ends. Nancy clapped. She was glad people could have fun with their bodies. Creativity was the best part of humankind, she thought. No other animal came close. She laughed, imagining the cats and dogs around the neighborhood and in her mind, she put mustaches under their noses.

After Nancy had finished playing Beethovan's "Moonlight Sonata," her teacher said, "Your playing is much better this week. Surprisingly fuller. Richer. Do you hear the difference? The most important part of playing profoundly is inhabiting your authentic self."

He took her hand in his and pressed lightly on the skin, looking out the window, as if he was distracted and didn't care what was going on. Then, he looked her deeply in the eyes, breathed deeply and lovingly, then pressed slowly down on her palm. "Feel the difference?"

She pulled her hand away to blow her nose and wipe her eyes.

"Nancy. If your whole self is on your team, you can do anything. You can be a hero."

"I know," Nancy said. "You told me."

"You've got the skill." He shrugged.

"I'm rusty."

"It's not the skill you need more work on." His eyes didn't let her look away from his gaze.

"Still more authenticity?" Her nose dripped.

"You got it."

"I can't wait." And underneath her snarky tone, she meant it. Something to hope for with all her might.

CHAPTER FOURTEEN
The Report

Nancy took half of a pill at dawn, as she couldn't stand to wait until her usual scheduled time. She had to get herself together for D-CIDE. She was actually glad this time it was Monday and she was well enough to go back to work. She could focus on finding her brown taupe dress and putting her luscious transparent pinkish gloss on her lips, drinking lots of water to make them plump out and look inviting to Julio. She scrubbed her face and used an astringent, detangled her hair, framed her eyes nicely with kohl, hoping Julio would show up to deliver a package to the office that day.

She would get caught up with her project after taking more days off than usual. Work would be hectic, and she gnawed on the details, all the figures and charts she'd have to make, the tables and forms representing dead ants, mice, pigeons, raccoons, snakes. Being part of that destruction made her feel like a serial killer.

Nancy bit her lips and chewed on the inside of her cheek. It had lines on each side that hurt from sucking in her skin. It got even worse when she ate gluten by mistake and her membranes swelled. She couldn't remember if she'd eaten any lately.

She did feel very weird. Her mouth seemed swollen. Trying to figure out her life, she assumed she'd just been sleeping a lot recently. As the day went on, she knew she'd been sick from withdrawal from the pills, but she couldn't remember what the symptoms were, other than nausea, weakness, and transitory hallucinations she forgot about when she took the Jollys again.

Still, something about becoming more authentic as she played the piano seemed to be making the hallucinations live just under the surface this time, instead of buried so far below her conscious self.

She didn't remember where she got the bruises days before. Candle wax had been stuck to her eyebrows. And on her thigh was something resembling encrusted semen. Repulsed, she scraped it off. Was she promiscuous when she sleepwalked? Was she into sadomasochism?

There was a little girl's ring on the floor. She started over to the drawer where she kept her smutty books and clothes, though she didn't remember what they were about anymore. She didn't want to admit it, but she wanted to see what would happen if she looked at the books. Would the depravity turn her on? How disgusting. Treating people like objects, women in the slave trade, having to pose rather than live with dignity. She was too scared to know how she would react.

Sometimes she smelled like someone's cologne. And it gave her a tingle. That tingle was the most disturbing of all.

All she knew to do was to take her early morning bath, long and hot, to sink into the oily sheen of lavender and bergamot, close her eyes, and sigh. She'd ride the sighs, deliberately smiling, and imagine flying away. Imagine being in a children's story in which flying was just the way things were done. Beautiful things. Dignified things.

She was flying out of the dull gray sky into one where the sky was a fabulous saturated blue, beyond anything she remembered. She remembered so little of her life. So very little. Almost nothing at all…The sky went indigo and dark, darker, completely gone beyond…

Slsssriglobunormflbbb.

***

Emily floated in the watery world brilliant with blues and violets, peaches and pearls. The fountain flooded into it, and the red rocks around the shore were light as a feather. When she walked on them, they lifted and fell, and slid across the ethers to the red buttes nearby. The moss breathed in and out, snoring a little until she watered it from the spring with her little watering can. Then, the moss was greener again and loved her more than before.

She didn't have Dog, so she was asleep and dreaming, inaccessible, off-duty. She and the toy were inseparable. Dog was her one true friend. She couldn't imagine waking up to a world without it and the tune it played that she could only hear when she slept. The tune which stopped the moment she opened her eyes.

She could do anything she wanted and have all the adventures she wished when she dreamed. She didn't have to think about all that complicated Enochian stuff for a while. She could run and jump off the cliff and fall until she almost reached the rocks below sticking out of the water like knees. She wouldn't land and smash, her *self* leaking out. She wouldn't drain into the ground, swirling into the inner tubes and passageways and the ocean out beyond.

No, she would sing her secret song, and that would make her fly back up, along the cliff face away from the rocks below. That wonderful swoop and soaring, like a water bird, that beautiful light as she flew facing the sun. The brightness flooding down on her, making her skin warm.

148

But, somehow, not warm enough. She was cold, too cold. Did the sun not love her?

**

Nancy came back to herself and opened her eyes, remembering where she was. The water was cool, and she rushed to get out and dry herself in her brown towel.

When she turned on the heat and saw the clock, she gasped, as she had to prepare quickly for work or she'd be late. She didn't remember why she didn't want to ever see her uncle, but she desperately hoped he didn't pop into D-CIDE. Some vague, incomprehensible things peeped their heads from behind the door. Others were reflected in the mirror on the door. Others were reflections in a fun house endlessly repeating and changing her appearance in all of them, different one to the next, changing as she wanted, liquid, flowing, the rectangular tunnels of repetition echoing backwards in all six sides.

She shook her head. She just couldn't ask him what happened to the XXX. She practiced how she would ask Martha. She and Martha had sung at the top of their lungs at karaoke many times, getting tipsy, skipping with their arms around each other as they walked to the bus. *There's just no way she could lie to me if I ask her directly. I'll ask Martha when Julio's there. He'll see me being brave. He'll like me. He'll be proud.*

It had been days without getting the chance to wag her tail when Julio came into the office for a delivery, giving her sly flirtatious looks. Maybe he would one day ask her out. She planned how she would go fill up her cup with water when he came in and be in the hallway with it as he left. Alone together. Maybe that's all she needed. Just a chance.

She'd gone without a bra one day the week before, so he could see how naturally perky her breasts were. She'd gone without shaving under her arms for a week so he could smell her pheromones. She'd worn earrings shaped like kissy lips. And double lip plumper. She enjoyed her life without needing a man. But, it had been a long time since she'd dated. *My skin's feel-good nerves are probably atrophying. It's for my body's sake I want him to hug me. For purely medical reasons.*

She'd forgotten about the encrusted semen already. She remembered some strange things, but she could forget about it and be part of the regular world like everyone else. She was ready for love. Even a day of it would be enough to make her feel like she really wanted to be alive.

When she arrived at work, she tried catching people's eyes, but no one responded. At this point, she almost wished Geoff *would* come into the office so she could read his face and guess if he'd been warning her. She didn't want to draw attention to herself by staying away from the office for too long. She looked around to determine if everyone else was ignoring what happened with the XXX or if the whole place was some kind of Mob company and she hadn't known.

She was ready to act. To risk her life on the information she already had. Julio would like her for that. If her uncle punished her by trumping up charges, or her career was ruined, well, so be it. She planned to stop taking the Jollys again the next morning. *I can't remember what the side effects are so they can't be that bad. I'm going to live authentically and take a stand. No, who am I kidding? I'm going to fry! Seriously, what was I thinking, busting my own boss? No, no, I have to stop thinking that way.*

She sat up straight, cleared her throat, used her deepest, most assertive voice, and asked the saleswoman, "Say, what happened to the module out back? If the rules got changed about dumping, it seems like the execs would be celebrating with champagne all week."

The saleswoman wiggled her hips, saying, "Yeah, and Mr. Buzner would have bought Martha a new Caddy and pearls by now."

"Where is Martha?" asked Nancy.

"No one's heard from her yet," answered the saleswoman.

"I hope she's OK," said Nancy and the manager at the same time. Nancy almost said, "Jinx" but thought better of it. Martha had skipped days at work before without calling in. Nancy already had learned how to take over some of Martha's duties. Martha wasn't indispensable. The gossip was always that she was there to keep the boss happy.

"Give her a few days," said the manager. "Martha's always pulled through out of her little spells before."

"Was the XXX taken to the dump?" asked Nancy, emboldened. She held her head high. She couldn't believe she'd come out and said it.

"He took his ex-wife to the dump!" proclaimed a laughing voice from the back of the room.

"No, seriously. Or was it exported to another country? What happened to it?" Nancy felt as if she were riding a wave in the ocean.

The saleswoman said, "Listen, cookie. Forget it. Who cares? Talking about it could jinx it. Any way that it's gone is *good* gone. Right? Most pretty women your age couldn't care less about things like that. Get a life. Get a man."

"Are you saying . . .?" Nancy's face burned.

The manager cleared her throat and everyone got quiet. All the woman needed to do was project a subtle glare, even from the back of her head, and no one spoke. She didn't seem to be in her playful mood.

As Nancy passed by Martha's desk, she noticed a felt tip pen that was labeled Sky Blue. Nancy swiped it and scribbled with it on some scrap paper at her own desk. She couldn't see a thing. How strange. She put it in her pocket.

She was determined to take only a half a pill that evening. The headaches were getting better.

During her first break, Nancy went to the lone remaining "dinosaur" pay phone in the neighborhood. It was near the bathrooms at the gas station down the street, which had some food she got for lunch sometimes. She didn't want her number to be traced when she called the police.

"I want to report an illegal dumping." She explained about the XXX and asked for anonymity. She said she'd call the police back the next day, Tuesday, to check on the results.

She'd done it. She really had.

CHAPTER FIFTEEN
Test Results

Early the next morning, when Nancy lifted the piano lid to play the song from her childhood, she found another note in the harshly angular, heavy handwriting. It said, "We're dying. Love us, don't kill us!"

She shut the lid immediately.

She paced around the apartment. She looked for any other changes she might not have noticed. She did a double take. There was no little box. Dog was gone. How long had the music box toy been gone and she just hadn't noticed? She muffled a scream.

She wanted to go for a run to disperse the nervous energy, but she was scared she'd be attacked. She closed the curtains and turned off the lights, opening them to peer through without being seen. She wished for a gun: she ate two candy bars in a row and felt sick. That was more her style.

She wanted to take the rest of the pill from the night before, but she kept to her resolve. She wouldn't take any that evening. She hoped to get in at least one full day of work before the symptoms came on too hard. She dutifully went to work.

She heard heavy footsteps coming down the hall at D-CIDE and her stomach jumped. Was Geoff coming in? The door opened, and it was instead only the manager of the manufacturing plant. She rubbed her abdomen, trying to get her stomach to normalize.

She waited until her morning break to call the police from the pay phone to find out the results of their test. She thought about mentioning the notes and the break-in. But that nonsense would have ruined her chances of getting them to believe her about the dump. She was startled when the officer said, "We detected zero molecules of XXX anywhere at the dump. If it had been poured out there, we would have found it immediately in the air. Our equipment is top notch."

She gasped. The police were in on the cover-up!

She went back to the office, but she couldn't stop thinking about it.

She wanted to do a search for local police corruption but didn't want her search history to show up on her computer at work. The police must have been bought off to hide the illegal dump. *Anyone can be bought.* Even the officers she needed to trust to keep her and everyone else safe were in on the conspiracy. Damn.

She wanted to call them back and tell them she knew the XXX was there. There were no records in the office of the chemical being shipped to another country, or any profits coming from that, and there was instead a record of the module being returned to the storage company. So, the cans had to be seeping death into the dump.

On her lunch break, she went back to the phone booth. She used the torn, dirty book to look up a man with a private company to hire him to test the air. She didn't want to be tracked, especially as Geoff might be on the lookout for her following up on reporting it in spite of the escalating warnings.

She requested the man's service that day. He was to go to the dump and have the answer ready for her by 5:30, at his place.

She saw a shadow flit around the corner of the gas station. The silhouette of someone's body disappearing behind it into the darkness. She wanted to get out of there immediately. Was it another warning? She took on a karate stance to at least scare the potential attacker. The street lights were dim enough she couldn't make anything out.

She wanted to buy something to eat so she'd look legitimate when she got back. The saleswoman had asked her to bring her a fried pie. She turned around and went into the store, never turning her back to where she'd seen the shadow. She sped to the fried pies and then couldn't stop herself from rationalizing. She needed to take what was closest to her and get out of there: a fabulous looking pastry with a power she couldn't deny.

When she left, she saw something disappearing around the corner again.

Back at her desk, she started eating the pastry, making herself take only a bite at a time, savoring her treat, hoping she wouldn't have much of a gluten reaction and go crazy. She kept thinking about the shadowy person at the gas station. Could he have been just a regular customer buying gas, going to the restroom and returning the key? She tried to tell herself that's all it was. But she couldn't shake the feeling someone had been listening.

Gorgeous Julio walked in with the day's packages. He looked at her with a bushy black eyebrow raised. She licked her fingers to get the sticky goo off them, trying to do it in a fetching way. She could already feel herself bloating from the gluten. She knew she was pasty and moonfaced, her skin pushed out and the pores looking bigger. Her lips were crusty and dry, her left eyelid sagging. She kept looking away from him so he'd look away from her, but his gaze persisted. She wanted to tell him she was a troublemaker. He should admire her. He should want her.

He nodded, jerking his head to the side, as if signaling he wanted to talk to her in the hallway. He looked serious, as if he wanted to ask her a question. But, she was starting to itch, and her vision was blurring. The walls were already starting to move, and she wasn't sure why there were so many skulls on the floor, with worms sliding out of them. She couldn't believe she'd eaten gluten after being so good at stopping the pills. One toxic overload at a time, girl!

He mouthed some words she couldn't make out. Something like: "Are you OK?"

But she was too embarrassed about how she looked to go to him. And anyway, all her brain could handle, without going into overload at that moment, was the vague notion of some secret room, with "the secreter room" inside it, inside her head.

It had to be a dream. Yet, it seemed she really had seen it. Somewhere. Not very long ago at all.

The effects of the pills were lessening. The effects of her authenticity practice were gaining. She knew she'd remembered much, much more when she'd gone off the Jollys entirely for days. She'd forgotten what she learned. But, even when taking partial pills, she had vague glimpses of new memories that made no sense. The worst was that her friend Jeff seemed maniacal to her, as if he was hiding something sinister, and she didn't want to talk to him.

She didn't want to dream about him or ever see his bewildering messages on social media again. She was done. He was a jerk who stubbornly wouldn't admit the truth about government programs. So there.

After she got off work she went to a vegan restaurant for dinner. She still had time to wait before the man would be done with the test.

After her meal, she drove to his house to pick up the results.

He was pulling into his driveway in a muddy truck. He looked trustworthy, like someone from the country, wearing overalls, a cap, and wire-rimmed glasses. He had a warm smile and gave her a firm handshake.

"Nothing there," he said. "XXX was not dumped there. I guarantee."

Had it been exported to a poor country instead to use in their pesticides?

She thanked him after paying him his fee for several hours of work. It was worth knowing the police weren't lying to her. She had been on a wild goose chase all along; the crime she thought had been committed had not been. She wanted to find out what did happen to the XXX. But, that would mean looking deeper into Geoff's mind to try to figure out what he might have been thinking. Who he might be colluding with. And why.

CHAPTER SIXTEEN
The Hunt

Angela Ageless ran through the darkness, the mists washing her face clean, her sheer black dress drenched in sweat, the lights around her jumping in her vision to the bounce of her high-arched footsteps, their golden glow unable to warm up the silvery fog of Angela's fears. She had to protect Emily. She *would* find her, had to help her grow up, had to help her escape, to twist and turn and plunge to hide below the surface or climb a tree or throw her whole self into something different that could not be named. Emily must not die. She. Must. Not. Die.

She turned left, ran until the left turn seemed like right, turned into forward going backward in a maze of oceanic chemicals wearing off, into the invisible walls that kept her secret, kept her from fading into someone else. Where was Emily, how could she reach her, how could she keep her from dying before it was too late?

If Emily died when Nancy's chemicals from the pills left her system entirely, died before Nancy remembered the childhood song that would help her put the pieces of the puzzle together, that would be the end of it. Nancy would never remember fully enough to become her authentic self. Poor Nancy. Angela wished she could hug her.

Angela had been created to keep the U.S. financial hegemony intact. She wasn't created to revolt. Nancy was looking into the parts of herself she had ignored before, deepening to love and music. And she was drawing on reserve parts of her that had been underground. She was finding out about Crank, Geoff, and the Intelligence mind control programs that had for decades been splitting people's psyches to make them into special agents. She was going to piece it all together soon, and if she didn't have the song as her lifeboat, she'd sink into the deep waters of nonsensical oblivion.

Nancy might kill people through the bottling plant if she became only the shell of herself without Emily and Angela to balance her selflessness. She just needed to work the last stage of production at the factory before the water was cleaned and before it reached the bottles.

If her alters died before Nancy remembered the song, Nancy could do nothing to rescue Emily and Angela from the prisons of their lives. Nancy could never understand what they had been forced to do. Nancy could never stop the handlers who made her alters do those wrong things Angela wanted to escape from. Angela wanted to break free, her light bursting forth into Nancy's veins. Angela desperately wanted her to love her even though she'd been bad, so very, very bad.

Angela panted, ran until she could no longer run. She crouched down to the dirt by the sidewalk, heaving, her face next to some stranger's collection of used condom packets laid out on the concrete, each one a different brand, torn plastic displayed in an elaborate mathematical design.

She couldn't risk the repercussions of any more handwritten notes, and definitely nothing so blatant as to write that Nancy should take her pills. If Geoff or Crank found notes like that, she'd be punished. Yet, what to do?

Nancy wouldn't make enough progress in becoming her authentic self if she kept taking the Jollys. Nancy *had* to remember the rest of the song before the chemicals left her body. That was all there was to it. She had to, had to, had to.

How many people in the world live in denial of parts of themselves they need to accept? How much richer would their lives be, if they inhabited their whole selves?

Nancy was so different from Angela, sexually pristine and modest. Angela felt the shame of her sensuous manipulations down deep. But, she shook it off, curled down and buried her face in the dirt by the sidewalk, lifted up and spit out grass dirty with dog shit, cat pee, bugs and tears.

But, with Emily, there was hope: that lucky girl who never had to do what Angela did — seduce men she'd prefer instead to go home with to watch a sunset. That little girl never had to face that the poison she bottled would kill whomever the Nevermind wanted.

Emily was like the darling members of the church, ecstatic in glossolalia celebration of life, devotion, and the glories of existence. She thought the game was fun. She didn't understand her fighting skills were real. She thought it was like fighting a make-believe pirate in a dream made of paper and talking animals. And flying through the sky on a flamingo. Playing with paper dolls. Enochian chess for fun.

How would Angela explain trauma-based mind control creating Dissociative Identity Disorder? Angela wanted to fix her and get rid of all Nancy's problems.

Angela wanted to *kick* her. Wanted to show her what life was really like for people like herself who didn't have the luxury of being protected, didn't have someone taking care of her and letting her play in a room full of illusions hanging from the ceiling, like a baby's mobile.

She cut herself instead, with the sharp edge of her ring. She bled. She licked the blood and smeared it on her face in

160

lines across her cheekbones. She walked, rangy, her shoulders high, her stride long through the drizzle, turning to rain, to a downpour that purified her face of dirt and blood, her dress of semen and cement, her mind of everything but the need for sleep, dreaming of Nancy, and the answer to how they could reach her.

Nancy, Nancy, Nancy. Oh, how Angela loved her. Precious one. How she wished she could *be* her. Julio would hold her if she survived, if she stayed out of prison, if she could stand who she was — Angela, awful Angela, her head held high in the rain, car lights making the lines of water into silver daggers of desire.

CHAPTER SEVENTEEN
The Tune

Julio looked at Nancy meaningfully the next day at work. Really, if she was honest with herself, he was the reason she was still going to the office. She wouldn't do it, but wanted to take her pills, so she could forget everything that took her away from him, so she could function and get a chance to see him. Yet, she was a screwed-up chick. She didn't even know why she woke up bloody, with wet hair that morning. But, this time, she had a vague idea. For the first time in her life, she'd caught herself in the wake-up phase, halfway in between. And in that state she'd glimpsed something. Another part of herself that had been coming through in waves and receding, in and out, for days.

She hadn't been sure she'd make it for her Wednesday shift without the help of any pills, but she was managing it. There was less to detox this time. Before, the memories had flooded in as the chemicals had left. Now, those memories seemed to be gone. But, she knew something was wrong. She knew she was not who she had thought she was all her life. And she knew it had something to do with Terry Crank. And something to do with espionage.

She was nearly as bloated from gluten as the day before, with granules under her eyelids, and bad breath, but she went to Julio in the doorway to the room when he nodded. She followed him into the hallway.

She had to admit that not only the gluten was getting to her. The withdrawal symptoms also made her face pale, the bags under her eyes dark, lips ghastly. She hadn't even brushed her hair that day, and it was matted from her rolling around on the bed all night, with no sleep.

Hallucinations of a little girl named Emily flashed into her mind. She didn't know what it meant. She knew she used to make up vivid stories as a child about Emily from the book and movie. But, that didn't mean she *was* her. She shook her head, and her glasses flew off. When she bent to pick them up, she felt her lack of grace, her weakness, her trembling, and the pain in her bladder making her wince.

She stood as far away from Julio as she could and still seem civil. Maybe distance would soften her appearance and her breath.

He reached out and touched her hand, drawing her a little closer. "That's great that you're looking into the XXX."

"How do you know I'm doing that?" Her mind was going fast. "I'm not going to talk to you if you won't tell me." She panicked. *Is he in on it? He's spying on me?* She reached out and held onto the wall. But, she wasn't going to budge. *How could he possibly know unless Geoff told him or he hacked into my emails, snuck into my house, or is a fucking spy?*

She turned away without saying anything to him and went back to her desk. Julio! Of all people to be on the other side. Pretending he was on hers. She rested her head in her hands on the desk. All that time, building up to talking to him and that's what he said. Letting her know he knew.

He kept hanging around the office, talking to people, looking over at her surreptitiously, his eyes narrowed. She wanted him gone. It was over.

What was? Nothing was there to be over. He delivered packages and she worked in the office and that was that. Her eyes stung. Her lips quivered. She wanted to throw her hole-puncher hard against the opposite wall. So hard it would break through the wall, all the way to hell.

"I'm going to take some packages to the gas station now," he said to the saleswoman. Been nice chatting." He walked out very slowly, pausing at the door.

Good riddance, thought Nancy. He was too young for her anyway. Why waste her beauty on a man who didn't have a professional career and a bright future ahead of him? What had she been thinking? Jerk. Shortie. Low life. Duckweed.

Ten minutes later, she saw him outside the door, positioned so most people in the office wouldn't be able to see him at that angle. He motioned to her to come outside.

She shook her head no and looked down at her spreadsheet. With her peripheral vision, she could see that he stayed there, hiding when anyone in the office walked past and could see him. The funny faces he made when doing so made her laugh. She covered her eyes with her hand, making it look as if she was keeping her hair out of her face.

She would have worn a plain ponytail to work to keep the other women from being jealous of her gorgeous looks. But, since she knew he'd be coming in from time to time, she always wore it down.

He leaped across the doorway, so she couldn't help but see him from her peripheral vision on the other side. She gave in.

"Cigarettes," she said. "Can't live long with 'em, can't live without 'em." She gathered up her pack and lighter and stood outside with him. "What?"

"I need to talk to you. Come on, don't be mad. I just took the packages across the street to the gas station. Look, that's also what I was doing when I overheard you on the phone. I didn't mean to pry. I just heard one sentence when I was walking around the corner to go to the bathroom."

"That shadow was you?"

"I wasn't sure I should say anything at first. I want to stand with you on this." He took hold of her hands and squeezed them gently.

She almost fainted with relief. She wanted to kiss him hard! *I love you!* But, she was a professional. Still, the fact that he got behind on his schedule meant he cared.

She said, "The thing is, I was chasing a shadow. It wasn't dumped after all. I thought maybe he sent it to another country that didn't have the same rules as here, but the profits don't show up on the books."

"Do you think Geoff could be selling it without reporting the profits to D-CIDE? Money laundering isn't unheard of, you know. And waste management companies tend to be corrupt. He could have bribed them to cover up where they transported it, no problem."

"Very possibly."

He leaned toward her and said into her ear, his breath moving her hair deliciously, "So, should you talk to the police about that?"

"Maybe. But to tell you the truth, I'm starting to wonder if it's something different. Something beyond their jurisdiction."

"What else would he do with it?" He was so handsome. His skin glowed in the sun.

"Well, it's the perfect murder weapon. It can't be traced. It can't be tasted."

"Hmm. You're saying you think he sold it on the black market?"

She nodded. "Or possibly stored it somewhere else. The cans might be too eroded and leaky. I know they'd break to pieces if they fell from a truck onto sharp things in a dump.

But maybe if they're treated well, they're still holding up. If not, I'd hate to be the person cleaning the module."

"God, I hope he told the cleaner about that if there was a spill!"

Will he admire my tenacity? "I've been looking into Terry Crank. You know, people say it's not just coincidence he's going to countries that have coups afterward. They say he's not just talking about God to all those world leaders he hobnobs with. Some women are accusing him of drugging them and making them do things. Some women are coming out about being mind-controlled Agents for the Nevermind programs. Couriers, things like that. They're naming Crank as their handler. They say he's involved in assassinations of leaders of countries who don't kowtow to the U.S. Agenda, and they're forced to help him."

"Fuck!" he said. "Are you serious? I've never heard of anything like that in my life. Do you think they're crazy?"

She studied his face. If he thought they were crazy, maybe he'd think the same thing about her. "He's never defended himself against those accusations. Wouldn't you, if you had a leg to stand on?"

"Hmm. I know the Nevermind is pretty weird. But, I don't know if I could take seriously someone who told me she'd experienced mind control by a Reverend." He laughed nervously.

Damn. She couldn't tell him. He'd never believe her. Maybe she could show him instead, and if he saw evidence first-hand . . . *If he believed me, would he stick around for a spy any more than if he thought I was nuts? If I did get out from under the control of the Nevermind, it would need to be as the acknowledged victim. Or witness of an unsanctioned crime that I could threaten to take public. I'd need to escape under a protection program. Change my last name. Move somewhere else, alone.*

She looked around and noticed that two men sat in an unfamiliar car in the parking lot, looking at her, turning their heads as she looked over.

"We need to get out of here." She took his arm. It was her first time touching him there, something she'd fantasized about all along. Her palm felt wonderful. The shape of his arm was perfect.

They got in his car. He started to drive recklessly, but she put her hand on his leg calmly to slow him down. *Two touches in one day!*

As they got out of his car when they arrived, she whispered, "Geoff is tied in with Terry Crank. I wonder if it might have something to do with him. And with the Nevermind."

"Why would poison have anything to do with an evangelist? That doesn't make any sense to me *at all*. A man of God? He's one of the most admired men in the world." He looked sideways at her, his mouth crooked.

She wanted to go along with what he said and not act crazy. She stuck out her rib cage to try to distract him with her form.

He smiled at her, crinkling his eyes, the sweetest moment she'd had while being made fun of. She could tell he thought she was adorably mistaken. She wanted to feel that way about herself, too. That way seemed to be leading to a kiss. She smiled back as if accepting and dismissing her indulgence in whimsy. She would forget all that stuff. Why did she care so much? She should just let it be.

She plumped her lips and sucked in her cheeks. She held in her tummy. She looked down at her bloated belly, at the evidence of her folly. She wondered if maybe in a few days when she looked more back to normal, she'd see if she could get him to kiss her. And in that moment, he kissed her.

She could hardly breathe. All right, the adventure was on. If he could look past how she looked and go along with her harebrained scheme, this could work out. They looked at each other. His eyes were shining.

"Wow."

Well, maybe he wasn't the most poetic person, she told herself, but "Wow" was how she was feeling too. She had to transition to business mode.

She added, "From what I read, he's not a snake handler himself, but his organization's main church is near here. It's huge. And it has a big congregation of snake handlers that go to it on Sundays."

"So?"

"You know a lot of them also drink poison, right? Or they used to until recently. I know a lot still do, in rural areas, but they probably couldn't get away with it here."

"I'm not getting the logic somehow. But, if you really think it might have something to do with Reverend Crank, we could go check it out."

"He's the main minister running it, but the deacons take charge when he's traveling. I don't know if he's in town now or not."

He smiled. "Great. Churches can be nice, especially big ones. And this one sounds pretty Southern Gothic with the snake handler stuff. I thought that tradition was dying out. Could be fun to see."

"It's still going strong, from what I understand." She tried to sound calm like a regular person with only a healthy passing interest.

She welcomed spending more time with him, whatever it was. Not the way she'd fantasized going to a church with him for a big day. But, it would do. Stupid fantasy, anyway, really. "See you after I get off work?" she asked. "I'll meet you here."

He answered, "No. I mean, not right here. Someplace no one will see us."

She liked the sound of that and hoped he'd say it to her in other circumstances sometime. "How about at the gas station?"

"That's the last place."

He was right. She thought about it. "OK, how about by the rabbit hutch? You know where I mean?"

He nodded. "At a few minutes after 5:00? If I see someone watching, I'll just drive on." He reached out gently and touched her shoulder, his lips red and open.

When she smiled back, she could tell something in her was shining through: some essence. That had to be what he liked about her if he could see through her body's unflattering appearance.

She liked that. She liked that a whole lot.

When they met up after work, he drove her to the Church of Divine Rays. "I've only been inside a couple times for weddings. And never on Sundays. Sundays are for the snake handlers to use the church. I usually sleep through Sunday mornings. It's a thing I do. So, I don't know if they leave the door open or not on Wednesdays." She felt as if she were speaking double-speak. Some part of her seemed to have been in the church regularly.

He said, "So what do we do now that we're here? When I went to Methodist Sunday School, I mostly got into watching the Daddy Long Legs on the walls outside. That's what I remember about Bible Study." He made the Inky Dinky Spider movement with his hands.

"We explore."

"An adventure. I like that." He took her hand. The church was unlocked, with several cars in the parking lot, and some of the lights were on inside. When they walked in, they saw a light from a room at the other end of the long hallway. It was too far away to hear voices.

"What if they come out of the room while we're here? Or someone else comes in?"

"You can't get in trouble for just walking into a church," he said.

"You know, the Charismatic Movement branched off from the Methodists. They're Dominionists. Some of the Evangelists team up with politicians and ruin the lives of indigenous people. And they spy on them for the CIA and tell them how they'd respond in case of a U.S.-backed coup."

"Say what?" His face looked gorgeous when he was incredulous.

She wanted to forget about things like the Moral Majority and just focus on being sexy for him. But, she knew if he ever cared for her, it had to be for her whole self. Whatever the hell that was.

They stood in the hallway and she heard a noise behind the wall. The sound of a large thick spring. Something was knocking the spring around.

They walked past the odd noise, down the hall. It was a familiar sound to her. Then, something about it got to her. "I wonder what that was?" she said, going back to stand outside where the sound came from. She leaned her head against the wall of the hallway and listened to what was coming from behind it.

But she *knew* what it was.

It was Dog's spring.

WTF.

She searched for a doorway in the hall to go through so she could retrieve the toy, but there was nothing. She felt the wall along the church hallway for some secret passage entry, some window to access it, though Julio looked bewildered as to why.

"There's no way to get to it. That's odd. There's nothing behind the wall. But somehow, apparently, there is."

"Really. Why does it matter? Want to keep looking around the church?"

She could think of no rational reason to look for it, so she put her arms around him as he put his around her, and they walked on down the hall.

When they got close to the lit room at the back of the church, they heard voices. She couldn't make out much. Something about poison. About a cartel. Cursing and laughing. A man saying, "Ironic. We haven't used the rat poison on the damn rats in this building."

Another voice said, "Get on it today. We can't have them biting some kid."

"Why, is that worse than a snake?"

"It's not commanded by the Lord."

Julio whispered, "We snuck in here to hear them talk about a pest control problem? We could have heard that at your plant. Don't you ever get sick of that topic?"

"Wait a minute," said Nancy. "Wait just a minute." She leaned against the wall. "I'll bet a rat was playing with something behind the wall. That's why it was making that springy sound."

"Eating it is more like it."

She felt sick. Dog being gnawed. She wiped her eye, turning her head away from Julio. She knew something huge was going down. Something far bigger than her or her longing for romance, something that mattered to the whole world. And it was all tied up with Dog.

She had no idea how to get into what was on the other side of the wall. She took Julio's hand and walked back to where they'd heard the sound. That's all she could think about at the moment. If she'd tried to process any more, she would have been torn into pieces.

Then she saw him looking at her strangely. "What?" she asked him. She couldn't stop her fingernails digging into her thigh.

"What are you doing? You're staring? And pouting. Why are you making that face at me? The sexy toddler look isn't really my thing."

"I didn't know I was."

"Pretty cute music, huh?"

"What music?"

"Coming from behind the wall. Guess the rat must have gotten into a music box mechanism. Listen, are you OK? Seriously. Why is your voice so high-pitched?"

"I don't hear music. All I hear is the sound of a spring."

"You're joking."

She and Julio followed the springy sound, feeling the wall for abnormalities. Some secret door. Nothing. She was shaking, and he took her hands in his. She felt halfway between herself and a child.

"Listen, I know you're upset. I can see your heart beating so fast it's moving your dress around." He put his hand on her chest, the way her piano teacher had told her to press with her soul into the keys, deepening into the music, into herself, into feeling below the surface. "I'm here for you. Breathe deeply."

Then, she suddenly heard the music. It was as if stoppers had been pulled out of her ears when he asked the question.

She had no idea how she knew: indistinguishable in the wall was a door that could be opened through the right combination of a song made of Enochian words. She bent to the wall and softly intoned. The door opened.

She felt as if she were living two lives at once. She knew who she was. She was also a little girl who had gone through

172

that room before, seeing it with awe, like a great play room, filled with fantastical triggers of imagination that kept her entertained as she did what she was supposed to do. Her mission was not yet coming through into the Nancy part of herself that was wavering, wafting.

She was suddenly clear: the sky-blue upward triangle triggered becoming Emily at the appointed time that day.

The downward triangle was for the days to become Angela.

The double triangle when she was to be Nancy.

Nancy realized that Martha had regularly marked them on her calendar at work with the Sky-Blue marker and had hypnotized her not to consciously see them.

Martha!

She was involved in all this too? She didn't seem like she had the personality for it. Her friend Martha! How could that be?

"Record a video of this, Julio."

He got out his phone and clicked on the video feature. She toned the Enochian unlocking phrase.

When she saw the secret room, with hanging cutouts of archetypal 1950s spies, knives, Bennu, espionage code, and gauze, she froze. On each paper spy there was an Enochian phrase, a numerical cryptogram, and diagrams of lines moving at right angles. On the wall was a painting of Emily, the girl in the children's storybook and subsequent Ehroh movie.

The fan-fiction that Nancy once thought she had made up when she was young, and had later dreamed of, was illustrated in that painting in vivid color. Riding Bennu out the window, everything outside the bedroom window in color, everything inside black and white. Other children, her ostensible brothers and sisters, ran behind her toward the world of color and magical delight.

Memories returned of her uncle Geoff personally training her as a child how to fight. Not karate. Dirty fighting. He'd instigated it when he first gave her the box. He'd played with it, with her, many, many times. Popping it open, popping it closed. When Geoff had pushed Dog's head into the box, it had been a psychological cue: the part of herself he'd compartmentalized, and that part of her would go into her box as well. She could remember reams of Enochian code when she was in that part. And not a word when she was her regular self.

When the box opened, Dog would play that song. That song she used to open the door. The song she … what else? What else was it? It was a missing piece.

"Quick, can you take some pictures of this place?" she asked him. "I brought a flash drive to put them on. Once I do that, you've got to delete them, so it's not traced to you. You don't need to be involved in this."

"This? What *is* this?" he asked as he took the photos in all directions. She captured the images on the flash drive she'd brought from work.

She would tell him what was going on with the black bag job. A bit. But not yet. Not only because he might think she was mentally ill but because she actually wasn't. There was more to it than that. She studied his face, and his eyes met hers. She grabbed the nasty chewed toy. "Put it back in the box."

Julio kissed her. Slowly. Frenchily. Nothing else mattered at that moment. Even when she looked her worst, and was such a mess inside, he could be attracted. The kiss was gentle, yet forceful, and she responded, holding her hand against the back of his head, stroking his neck, dipping her little finger into the hole in his ear, making him moan.

When he slid his hand down along her back, she forgot about the tortured sexuality she'd begun to remember, and all that was washed away. She was again a woman in the moment.

The sound of footsteps and voices echoed down the hall. She shut the door, said, "Take off your shoes." They held their shoes and they ran.

The footsteps followed, speeding up. The couple fled faster. They held hands as they ran, and he was pulling her to help her keep up with him, giving her no chance to fall behind. They ducked inside a coat closet, pressing up against each other as the footsteps continued. She liked the moisture of his breath against her neck. She felt his heart beating against hers.

She was glad they'd driven his nondescript car and parked it far enough away no one would suspect her of being the intruder. Her breath came harder in such a small, crowded space, pushed up against him in the dark. He held her around her waist, and nuzzled her neck, and kissed her heaving collarbone.

When the coast was clear, they left, and she focused on his features, on pretending to be ordinary, in case he really couldn't accept her any other way.

When they parked next to her car in the parking lot, he took her hand as she started to get out, and drew her to him. "Can we have a date?"

She nodded. What had she been hankering for all along? It was finally happening. Nothing else took priority.

"Maybe tomorrow? It's my day off. I know your days off are different each week. Are you free during the day? Or if not, in the evening?"

She was flattered he'd kept track of when she was in the office.

"Yes, tomorrow day *and* evening!"

Nancy disabled her browsing history, set up an encrypted email and wrote to the contact info Brandon had on his site.

His site explained, "Use encryption or anyone could more quickly trace who writes to me. The contact info below is routed to a different email. I welcome messages, but don't guarantee I will talk to you. You must provide a photo of you holding an ID that you take at the time of each message, with a time stamp on it as an attachment. No shoes. I'll do a background check on you before even thinking of answering."

She took her ID out of her purse and took a webcam photo of herself holding it.

"I have a bodyguard near me at all times. If anything happens to me, information I hold back as a matter of national security will be automatically released to the public from various servers. Beware if I am arrested, hurt, killed, kidnapped, or detained in any way that prevents me from reengaging the settings, or if any of my contacts are."

She wrote, "I'm a fan of your work. Your videos about Terry Crank have been helpful to me in piecing together my life. I'm gathering information you might find useful." She typed so quickly she made multiple errors, and went back to fix them. She was glad they didn't go through. He would think she was insane. Was she?

Little time passed before his response. "Hello, Nancy. I have flawless virus protection. Nothing you send can hurt me. If you have real information, pass it along now."

After she sent attachments, labeling them as the Church of the Divine Rays, he wrote back, "Very interesting. What is it?"

"A secret room in Terry Crank's church. I'm the only one who can open it with the key, which uses DARPA's aural technology set to Enochian language in high tones. Some sound on the video is the aura key. If something happens to me, please use it to get inside. You can see the map I included of the church and the hidden door."

176

"OK?"

"I don't know what it's about yet. Child abuse, if nothing else. I want to establish contact with you now and send you more as I find out more. Will you accept it?"

"Assuming it all checks out."

"Thank you, Brandon. I'll be in touch." She sighed. Things were in movement. Forward momentum engaged.

CHAPTER EIGHTEEN
The Butte

Julio picked her up at 10:00. She was glad she was looking like herself again, even if she didn't feel like it. Surreal, foreign memories were creeping through her body, like an underground peat moss fire spreading from her vagina. She remembered being sexy as hell, with a sinuous way of moving, knock-em-dead confidence, and a voice like port wine.

When she walked out of her front door to his idling car, she naturally swayed her hips, and when he whistled, she gave him a look of intense passion that made him jump out of his car and open the passenger side for her, while the truck veered around him honking.

They kissed in the front seat as he began driving and wobbling in his lane, nearly bumping the car next to him. "Someday you need to move where you have a driveway or at least someplace to park in front of your place. You can't count forever on the times when the light is red up ahead."

"I doubt I'll be staying here long, anyway, Julio. I don't think I'll be safe once I bring Geoff down. He's got to have cronies here. But, let's keep in touch. Don't tell anyone, but I'm thinking of changing my last name to Hole."

"Nancy Hole? A little risqué, there, honey. How about Whole?"

"I'm feeling sort of a bit of both these days."

"Hall? Worhol?"

"You're missing the point."

"Hmm. We're off! Covered Butte, here we come!"

"Yeah, I need to cover my butt, that's for sure, if I'm going to get out of here alive."

He chuckled. "Sure. And to tell you the truth, I'd be honored to see your butt gloriously nude, my dear."

He let down the roof of his convertible as they got to the outskirts of the city, and the brisk wind made his cheeks rosy and his laugh staccato. She shook out her hair and let it whip around her face. She closed her eyes against it, opening them a little from time to time to see increasingly stunning scenery with the rocks reddening, trees becoming more gnarled as the road climbed onto higher ground.

They turned off onto a twisty road that curved around the edges, and she looked over, seeing a perspective she hadn't taken the time to explore before. The city was far enough away to be a memory of mundanity, her boring job and anxieties over survival seeming foreign to her as she felt the euphoria of the ride with the attractive man beside her taking the turns boldly.

With the speedy curves, her body angled towards his, and she felt the distance between them as if she were a sentient magnet. When they touched briefly with the strong turns in the road, she felt her skin become electric. When they reached a flat stretch, he put his hand on her thigh and she felt the warmth growing, making her pubic zone tingle, and her vulva open wide, feeling more inclusive than she remembered it ever being. Her sex felt like a force of nature instead of a source of insecurity.

She started to purr into the wind and laughed at the scrambled sound it made. She leaned over and purred into his ear instead, so he could hear the husky depth in her voice.

"You've changed, Nancy," he said.

She didn't ask if that was OK as she would have done before. She didn't try to change back to the uptight way she was before in case her sensuality was too much for him. "Hell, yeah, I have," she said instead.

And he said, "God, I think I love you."

Her chest pressed toward him on its own, her heart melting forwards like lava. She felt like only the seatbelt kept her from becoming such a fire she melted him too, creating a conflagration beyond anything she'd imagined love could be. She didn't care that it was temporary. Time was not so important. Space was not either. They would be connected beyond space and time, togetherness or "dating" even more that day, she was sure of it.

As they slowed and drove up to the low, mild butte which had a few scraggly trees holding onto the rock, she couldn't believe the majesty of the world she'd been living in, with something so amazing not so far from where she spent her days inside her apartment or the office. She stretched her legs which were stiff in the knees from the chill. He got blankets and a picnic basket from the trunk, and they walked to the butte, seeing no other cars parked in the small lot.

They scampered up until they found a good tree to lean against, and he set out the spread. They covered themselves with one of the blankets, huddling together as they unwrapped and ate the still-warm fingerling potatoes, swirling them in a minty chive dip. She breathed deeply as she surveyed the land below them and listened to the songbirds who were eating the red winter berries below.

She rubbed her hands together for the warmth and touched his face tenderly, looking into his eyes with a free-flowing vulnerability that made her heart feel more present than ever. She was changing indeed, remembering some part of herself that was sensual beyond measure, yet which had not been allowed to be honest and free. Had not been allowed to see into a man's clear eyes so deeply, leaving her own eyes unblinking, not looking away, not faking a smile, but just being.

She felt almost like a trusting child, at the same time as the surprisingly sensual woman. A magical child. Like what was happening was wondrous, beyond the constraints of reality adults put on things to dampen down their expectations. Like synchronicity ruled, not taxes and mortgages.

She leapt up and danced, he right behind her. He climbed into the wrinkled little tree, and she climbed the one close to it, as their combined weight would have been too much for its branches. They called to each other in a made-up language, not glossolalia, not Enochian, just nonsense for the pure enjoyment, speaking to each other with inflections like English, full of exaggerated meaning and emphasis, wildly gesturing with their free hands, their faux-discussion getting more heated in an increasingly ridiculous way until they couldn't help breaking the spell by laughing.

They moved to the branches closest to each other and each held on with one hand, leaning toward each other, hesitantly balanced, reaching their other hands out, trying to make their fingertips touch. When they did, she felt the magic. She felt his electricity flowing with hers. How much she wanted him, right then.

She coaxed him down to the ground, and on the blanket, she pulled off her thick pants and spread her legs boldly before flapping the corner of the blanket over herself. The day was growing full, the sun warming the rocks beneath her.

He jumped down, landing solidly on his feet with a thud. He stood over her, and she marveled at the perfection of his form. He took off his clothes, the sun coming out from a wispy cloud behind him, so she could barely look, but as she shaded her eyes she saw how much he found her appealing, too.

He descended upon her with skillful force and precision, and they made love between the blankets, between the songbirds and the vast expanse of the true and simple magic inherent in red rocks.

CHAPTER NINETEEN
Locks Unlocked

That evening, after dark, they drove back to the city to the church. Thursday was not an active evening. No lights were on, and no one in the parking lot. They tried the doors, but they were locked. Nancy felt around the front and back door for the Enochian lock, but felt only the ordinary kind. Julio went exploring and then called out from around the side. "Hey, this looks like that one did. It's got that sigil engraved in it and the silver disc that spins around. Check it out."

She went around the side of the huge church and looked where his flashlight was pointing to the old boarded-up well-house. It was locked, ostensibly for safety, no doubt. She pulled the square tin box from her bag and turned the lever. When the wet, grimy Dog popped out, she remembered the key. She intoned the Enochian words into the door and the lock shifted and opened. He popped Dog back into the box immediately.

She wanted to know what part of her was hiding behind Dog's song and the words it made her remember. What had Geoff done to her?

They opened the entryway and climbed down inside, stepping on rocks piled along the side of the well. The bottom had cold standing water that came up mid-shin. They felt around the walls of the well, Julio jumping with a little cry. "Spider bite," he said.

"God, I hope it's not poisonous."

He shone the light on it, but she couldn't tell.

"Here it is," he said, and pulled open a small square door that was chest-level. He lifted her up to it. She climbed inside the passageway as he came right after. They crawled, lifting their flashlights up and putting them down, out of sync, as they moved their hands along the damp tunnel with no light ahead. She felt claustrophobic and had memories of being tormented as a toddler by Geoff, being put in a box with Jeff, the lid closed, and left for three days during her Slain time.

She sobbed and wanted to hug Julio, but had no space to turn around. She needed to blow her nose but had no tissues. She got to the end, a solid wall. She couldn't stand the idea of backing up to get out, and not being able to go forward. She hyperventilated, and he held onto her so she didn't fall over. "I'm here, I'm here," he said. "Tell me soon what's going through your mind. You can cry on my shoulder all you want — once you can reach it, that is. Right now, feel for a door."

When she found the handle, all she had to do was open it, and she nearly fell through it, lunging forward. He grabbed hold of her arm as she felt the air in front of her, discovering a platform to crawl down onto. She wasn't sure what it was, or whether it would support her or roll out, whether someone was sleeping there, or if there was some horrible deterrent, like a sharp stake she'd land on.

When she felt around, as far as she could tell, the platform seemed safe. She helped Julio onto it as well. They shone their lights through the little room, one she recognized only with her body, not yet with her mind. It had been that kind of day.

They wandered around, not risking turning on the lights, but lighting the candles they found. He asked, "Do you think they'd notice if we lit the incense just a little bit? For fun?"

"I don't know. But, let's live dangerously… Just let it burn for a couple minutes."

The room was spectacularly beautiful, lushly painted, with red velvet chairs, the walls and fine antique desks full of intricate Enochian tables and charts, images of Osiris and Bennu, Isis and Horus, Golden Dawn and Crowley tarot cards, I-Ching layouts, astrology charts, alchemical drawings, geomancy and Qabalah notations, grimoires from Eliphas Levi and Abremehlin the Mage.

An Enochian Chess set was on display in the center of the room. The floor was painted entirely with sephiroths, watchtowers. Everything was marked with Enochian letters, which were supposedly scried by Edward Kelley as he stared in an obsidian mirror in Poland, creating incantations to summon the angels. Or so he told John Dee.

Julio stumblingly tried to read it aloud, making some progress, as some Enochian letters look and are pronounced like English.

She surprised herself with her knowledge when she corrected him gently, saying, "You read them right to left. It's still quite a bit like English, all right, more than Kelley and Dee would have liked to admit to their public. It's not a naturally formed language, from what linguists say. The phonetics are more like glossolalia, and some words are obviously based on English. If you ask me, it's pretty funny they thought they could get away with claiming it was real. But, magicians like to think it is. It surely has real effects for countless people. Supernatural effects."

The barriers were breaking down between her compartments. She was amazed to realize how educated she was. She'd thought she was bad at history.

185

"What was it for then?"

"Well, Kelley made a bit of change with it, and got some power, though not as much as when he turned into more of an alchemist." She was beginning to enjoy not taking pills and having so much esoteric knowledge at her fingertips. She was educated after all.

"So, if it's just all stupid fakery, why is there such a big deal made out of here? Whoever made all this can't be playing around."

"Dee used it originally for espionage purposes. Passing information to spies and all that. He and Sir Walsingham were in charge of the first real secret service, protecting the Queen and her empire that he basically suggested she create. Kelley said the angels would give them superhuman powers, and they would use Enochian to change the balance of power and make the empire. It worked, considering it was used as part of their Intelligence agency."

"OK. But what's the use of it now?"

"Lots of things, really. The Golden Dawn guys made the chess set to encode all the esoteric mysteries of their society. Like all the things you see here, astrology, alchemy, I-Ching, all of it was hidden inside the chess set. The chess set can be used for divination. Satanists use Enochian language all the time for their rituals. The O.T.O. and Crowley and amateur magicians use the magick all the time. Sort of like using the Tarot, you know, helps access the subconscious, helps focus for rituals, stuff like that."

"Do you like it? Is it nice?"

"It's supposed to be used to call in the angels to bring on the Apocalypse."

"Great!" He chuckled. He made a goofy face.

She wasn't feeling silly. "I don't know why, but it feels super creepy to me. Like something happened to me with it that was bad. I'm sorry to bring you into this. I'll find a way to protect you."

"What about for other people? Do you think Enochian is worthwhile at all? Like, should I pick it up? I feel like I'm learning so much and it's so beautiful here." He handled the objects one by one, shining the light on them, bending close to see the details. His eyes were open wide.

"People who use it tend to have freaky supernatural things happen. Dark things. It seems to *maybe* really work to call in the angels, even though in my opinion they didn't exist until they were — created."

"Can that happen?"

"I really don't know. But, you know, maybe. It's called making egregores. Tuplas."

"How strange."

"What's stranger is that I never studied this stuff. But, somehow I know it. I almost feel like I have an eccentric sexy auntie who knows these things instead of me. But, that's just weird."

He took out his phone and took pictures of everything. "Look at this!" he said. "Holy fuck! It's a painting of you. But, like a little girl. Hey, it looks like Emily from that movie. You know, the one Ehroh is making a sequel for now. This actually looks like the sneak scene from the movie I saw in an article about it last week. It's supposed to be made into a game too, did you know that?"

She sat down. The curved smooth arm rests on the chair felt familiar under her hands. She caressed them absentmindedly. She took a new flash drive she'd packed for the trip. "Can you put this in your phone? And after you upload the pictures, you have to promise me you'll erase them. When you give me the flash drive, I'll wipe off your fingerprints."

"You don't want me to get involved?" he asked.

"I don't want you to get dead."

"What's this all about, honey?"

"I think it's supposed to be used to mind control people. That's what the first movie was for, too. That's what Ehroh Productions are all about. And for mass propaganda. How strange that such awful people make such sumptuous movies out of Lookout Mountain Labs. It's not fair. It would be so nice to be able to just enjoy the movies and the games, instead of being taken into their worlds. Into the twilight world of the Nevermind."

"Look," he said. "A skull. It's kind of smashed-in on the side. Must have gotten it in the bargain basket." He grinned darkly.

"And it has a ruby embedded in the front right tooth." She stared, silently. "So did my father's. He was hit on the head right there at the end." She set her jaw, narrowed her eyes and clenched her fists.

"Are you saying . . . That's your father's skull?"

She stared in silence. She was beyond crying. He had been dead since her youth. She had suspected Crank more every day. Now, she had something like proof. "Take pictures of that from every angle, Julio. Please."

"Wow, you're a hell of a date. Is it like this with all the guys?"

When she didn't say anything, he said, "Sorry." He knelt next to her, his hands on hers, and just breathed with her.

"It's OK. Really."

"Let's find that room you wanted to get back to," he said finally, breaking the velvety silence.

They felt their way down the hall to the spot where the secret room lay behind the wall, the door imperceptible. She didn't remember exactly where the entrance was, the lock being flush with the wall and painted to match. But, feeling around for a while, she found the minuscule indentation.

Julio recorded video to save the audio key again and opened Dog's box. When Nancy fluxed into Emily, fluttering between personalities, she intoned the Enochian words, her lips near the wall. She moved, bent down, repeating it all along that spot in the hallway and then they heard the little buzz and click and the door opened.

Julio closed Dog's box again to normalize Nancy, and they went inside.

The absurd room inside, with paper spies covered in sigils hung with thin lines from the ceiling, looked even more bizarre by flashlight. The spies spun in the breeze from the door opening, their whiteness flashing in and out of the silvery beam, casting shadows on the ones behind, reflected in the mirrors on the sides.

With so few chemicals from the pills moving through her bloodstream, the room looked somewhat familiar, though she didn't know what it was for, beyond espionage theater.

She studied the picture of herself on the wall, dressed as Emily flying through a window, the part of her body inside the room in black and white and the part of her body outside the window in color. Just like the fantasy stories she used to think she wrote when she was a child. It was the story in which she rode on Bennu the flamingo god from the movie she'd watched over and over as a child, with Geoff holding her on his lap on visits to the family, babysitting her when her parents were gone.

She flung her head against Julio's chest, making him stumble a step backward until she felt his strength push back against her, and his arms fold around her, making the flashlight beam circle the cutout in the room, with lint floating through the air.

He started to take a picture of it with his cell phone, and she put her hand over the lens.

"You might be in a lot of danger," she said. "Especially with a photo on your phone. Listen, you're dealing with a really fucked-up person right now. I didn't know. I'm sorry. I never would have let myself feel this way about you if I had. You might want to leave."

"No, are you kidding? Come on, girl."

"I don't know the Enochian to get inside, but look at this."

Her arm reached out without her even knowing exactly why and pushed aside the picture of herself flying out the window. There was a door. She beamed when she found the little girl's ring inside her pocket and pushed it into it. The sigil fit perfectly. She twisted it and then pulled away. She pushed, but only the first part of the lock was undone. She needed the tones to finish it.

But she could only remember the tones, special notes, not only the words, when she was having an orgasm.

She put her hands around Julio's neck and drew his face to her with some force.

He returned the passion and tightened his grip on her exquisite body. He pushed her up against the mirrored wall, and she watched them in the opposite mirror reflected endlessly as he took off her clothes. He undid his pants and proceeded to make love to her fast and furious, steaming up the mirrors and her memory.

"Turn on the recorder!"

"That's kinky." He did.

They came together and at that moment she cried out the sound of the Enochian key, the door to her right opening with a purring sound. She reached over quickly and stuck a folded piece of paper inside the door, sticking out halfway in case it might close.

They panted, holding each other, kissing and caressing, catching their breath. They cuddled for a long time, she running her fingers through his thick straight hair, he counting aloud, touching the moles on her back which he labeled a constellation. She felt more like her whole self than she ever had. Only sharing some of it with him and having him stay would make it complete.

"I'm sorry to bring up something icky after that. That was beautiful, Julio. I want to be close to you. I want to be honest. It's just. I should tell you I was abused as a child. I flew away from it by picturing this window and riding my torment into the blue. I went into the Nevermind."

He kissed her fervently, and said, "I love you. All of you."

And that opened up more of her mind than anything else had before.

They climbed into the even smaller room, which was very tiny and filled with little funnels and bottles without labels, poison rings and flasks, squirt bottles and water guns, as well as spy tech of all shapes and sizes. Protective gear lay in the corner, shaped like the Bee of Ra.

Then she noticed. The tight walls were not walls. They were stacks and stacks of cans of XXX on one side of the wall. A stack of new various-sized containers on another wall. And two walls were metal boxes.

Perfectly lined up from the floor to the ceiling, all the way around, they formed a prison of death. This was where the waste truck had taken the chemicals. No wonder they had avoided her chase.

The waste company had not reported transporting it to Crank's Church of the Divine Rays. Thus, Geoff's prerogative in his new job: oversight.

Julio took photos and passed them to her flash drive. She had the evidence as long as she could report it without being caught or killed, without it being stolen first. She could continue to hover. But, who could she report it to? It was

Nevermind business. She'd keep Julio out of it if she could manage it.

She was getting somewhere. But, this was not what she had expected.

"Please take me home."

They drove in silence for a long time, he putting his hand on her leg with a subtle nuance of pressure. She felt the energy from his hand sink into her.

"I'm sorry for what we found. I don't understand it." His face was contorted. "I don't like where this leaves me legally, babe. You knew where the poison was. Your picture was in there. The evidence seems to show that you are part of an illegal activity that probably involves murder. Right? But, what the hell?"

"I know." She could barely make out what he said next in the wind, the convertible top down under the amazingly starry sky. His voice wafted to her in fast waves.

"I can't condone murder." His voice was gravelly. He turned his head toward her and his eyes were narrow with obvious emotional pain. She felt terrible seeing how he felt hurt, betrayed, and as if he couldn't trust her. She didn't want him to push her away. But she wouldn't blame him if he didn't stay with her even another minute.

She said, "I can't either. I wouldn't want you to. Stopping the crimes; that's the point, isn't it? Even if I did them."

"Does that mean I'm supposed to turn you in? I should. But I don't want to do that!" His reddening eyes looked like they were watering and stinging. He hit the steering wheel, which set off the alarm. He struggled to turn it off quickly.

"No, it doesn't. I'm going to turn myself in." She looked ahead resolutely.

"I'm sorry." He looked straight ahead at the road too, she could tell out of her peripheral vision.

"I didn't do it consciously, believe me. It's like somnambulism. Was made to do it." She held her head in her hand.

He was silent as she watched his face. She was afraid of what he was going to say. Finally, he said, raspily, "I believe you." He still wasn't looking at her.

She wanted to take his face in her hands and turn it toward her even if it made him swerve. She wanted to see the look of love. Not pain.

"I feel horrible." She held back tears until she felt one drop on her knee. That tiny drop felt so sad to her she sobbed one time, then pinched herself until the intensity of the pinch overcame her self-indulgence.

"What will happen?"

"Definitely a cover-up. But, if I catch them at something that goes beyond what they have to do for their job…"

"Catch who?" He looked at her, but it didn't feel like enough. She wanted more.

"Uncle Geoff. Terry Crank. Man named Jeff: they screwed him up bad."

"What happens if you stop doing your job with them? Will someone else step up?"

"I'll throw a wrench in their plans." She tightened her lips.

"I don't think any one person can change the system."

"I know. And without a plan in place to replace it, all I would do would be create chaos if I did. The lifestyle of every man, woman and child in the States depends on the Nevermind to keep the war machine going and keep the petrodollar king of the hill."

"If you pulled the plug out all the way, there would be anarchy in the streets."

She sat in silence. She hated the sniffle she couldn't hide well enough by clearing her throat. She was the bad guy. She had done horrible things. What right did she have to cry?

As he pulled up to her apartment he said, "We live in kind of a Noir world, don't we?"

As she got out of the car she countered, "I'm going to make my life better in the long run. I want to try to bring some awareness of at least the XXX. I have the evidence now of where it is. But, not yet where it's going. It's got more than one purpose, right? You can tell by all the different types of containers I put it into and all the different packaging."

He got out and walked over to her. "Well, all I can say is, hello to the rest of you. Do you understand that what happened isn't your fault? You can't blame yourself." He tipped an imaginary hat and then gave her the longest, most inclusive hug she had ever experienced.

She let a tear stream down. "I can't say how much I appreciate that. Don't know when I'll see you again. Or if I will."

"It's OK. It will be OK."

He drove away, his breathtakingly dark hair turned into a halo by the incandescent street light ahead.

Once home, Nancy contacted Brandon again.

"Inside a room beyond the secret room are containers of a poison banned a long time ago. XXX is perfect for murder, working immediately if ingested and more slowly if on the skin, in which case it maims but does not necessarily kill. It's tasteless, invisible, and leaves no trace. As you see, it's being put into numerous types of containers and none of them is for pesticide use. The video I uploaded contains the sound to open the door."

In about five minutes, she got the reply. "Good material, Nancy."

"And I maybe can't prove Geoff Buzner killed my parents, but at least there's grave-robbing. My father's skull was in the church."

"For ritual use?"

"Yes."

"I'm sorry to hear it."

"I'm a cutout for the Agency. I wouldn't have been a good one without Geoff taking over my training full time." She wasn't sure she should be writing this to him. Surveillance was very good. Who was logging her keystrokes?

He gave her his phone number and told her to write or call when she knew more. "Carnivore will get a kick out of our COMINT. Whether it's cleartext or not, they'll know eventually. Everything we do sends a message. It's up to their conscience what they do with it."

"Those who do wet work tend to end up drenched."

"We'll see, Nancy. We'll certainly see."

CHAPTER TWENTY
Dying into the Abyss

Emily and her Auntie Angela lay in the double bed all that night, clasping each other tightly, their legs and arms intertwined, their cheeks pressed against each other, their energy flowing into each other, hidden from Nancy inside her Nevermind. They were each other's breath.

Angela whispered to the little girl who struggled to hear her, twisting and turning her face to position her ear near Angela's mouth but finding her neck in pain, the ligaments reaching their limits, the pressure of Angela's bony cheekbones bruising her flesh.

The mordent voice was never loud enough, or stable on one note, to catch everything. Emily had to piece together the words that bounced off the walls, reflected off the mirrors and spoke to her in rhyme echoing her own thoughts, but backward. "I know this sounds very odd. But, we're sleeping inside a woman's body. Nancy looks very much like we do. You've dreamed of her often, wondering who. She wears much more boring dresses than we do."

Emily tried to answer, but when she opened her mouth, the words came out of Angela's, with a higher tone. "I'm dying."

Angela continued, with her sultry sound. "Because Nancy has not remembered the three-part song that wakes us inside her. She's getting so close to embracing us all. Her personality is starting to include us. But, as the chemicals leak, the gaping abyss grows wider. We'll feel the pain of death when we fall."

Emily wiggled, trying to break free from Angela's grasp. She tried to cry, but the relief wouldn't come. The toxins flowed from Angela's tear ducts, and one warm drop landed on Emily's nose, making her jump. She gasped for air, and all that came in was Angela's outbreath, and she felt herself suffocating, felt the woman's grip around her body tightening, crushing her rib cage with pain.

All she saw was darkness where once was the light of dreams, and she heard the very sound of the widening abyss, a roar, a hiss, a screech, and darkness grew darker than she'd ever known possible.

Angela's feet grew so cold they became numb. She struggled, but she couldn't reach them to feel if they were still there. Her legs intertwined around Emily's; her feet were unable to touch each other to affirm their continued existence.

Below them came the breeze, up from the abyss. Angela felt its cold only in her calves, and then not even anywhere in her legs at all. She still felt the heat stir in her sex. She couldn't deny a longing to use her prodigious powers to please men for her own joy. She wanted to know love. To trust a male. To let out her celebratory pleasure yells for all the neighbors to hear.

Emily wished to grow up and take care of herself, to see what it was like not to be ultra-important. She wanted to understand the secrets the adults kept. Even the scary ones about how the world really worked. She longed to grasp the consequences of her actions. She wished she'd have a chance to use her magic to make wonderful things happen, to dance in just the right way to make the universe laugh.

Angela and Emily shivered, their goosebumps pushing against each other's amorphous skin inside Nancy's forgetting, as they faded away toward the enveloping darkness of nothing, forever and ever.

CHAPTER TWENTY-ONE
Snakish

Alyssa called Nancy, saying, "I got your voice mail from a few days ago. Yes, sure, I'm fine, and the trip was great. We just got in an hour ago and are sort of tired from the trip. God, I just wish it wasn't Friday morning already. Hey, guess what. I almost died!"

Nancy's hand trembled only slightly as she held the phone. Had Jeff tried to attack her karate partner as a warning? He was certainly at the same park at the time. She seemed to remember him making a threat years ago that he would kill Alyssa if Nancy screwed up. But, that made no sense. Nancy had only met him recently.

"I went out exploring around in the evening. I was walking along, away from everything in the most primitive part. I came up behind a slow man on a narrow path, trying to get past him, but there was a cliff on one side and an abyss on the other."

Nancy shuddered.

"When the trail widened enough that I finally could get around him, there was a rattlesnake, right there!"

"Oh, God!" yelled Nancy. Had Jeff arranged the whole thing? No, that was crazy talk. Old men hiked slowly on trails. Snakes lived in the forest. That's how it worked.

Alyssa said, "It rattled and was about to strike him. Know what I did? I distracted it and then it came at me. I killed it with my camping knife to keep it from biting him. He thanked me and went along his little old way. I skinned the snake and ate it." The phone made blips and scratchy noises, Morse code, and tinny sounds.

"Wow, girl. You strong!" She was always impressed by Alyssa's capability of living life to the fullest and facing it head on. Platitudes. All been done, all been thought. She could only barely feel the love for her friend. She loved the snake more, slithering along minding its own business, not cutting down trees to build a parking lot.

What right does Alyssa have to live at the expense of a snake in a park? Why's Alyssa so cavalier about taking down one of Earth's creatures?

Nancy always apologized and thanked her meat before she ate it. *We are all murderers here.*

She felt strange. Unreal. Too "thin," as the piano teacher said about her music. Not enough there. She bent to hold the receiver on her neck as Alyssa told her more adventures of living in the wild on her camping trip.

She felt her wrist for a pulse. It was febrile, or wiry. Too fast and surface. Where was the rest of her? She barely mumbled goodbye. She sat down. She was filling up the top of her lungs but not her abdomen.

She couldn't understand why she didn't care. In fact, she wasn't sure any of her friends really had a great need to live, as far as she was concerned. She found herself almost wishing the spider had bitten Julio so badly his arm would fall off from necrosis and he would die. Humans. Too many of them for the planet.

In waves, the convoluted and multilayered process of breaking through her trauma-based multiple-personality programming felt like life. One of those waves hit right after their phone call ended.

She emailed Alyssa. "Let's get together soon. I have some things I want to tell you. I don't want to talk about them online. And don't bring your cell phone, so no one listens in. But, you need to know I'm not what I seem." She so wanted to talk about phone surveillance and not sound like a wingnut.

The message bounced. It was said to be undeliverable. But, why? Had someone intercepted it? A warning?

She felt as if she were falling apart, and nothing could ever put her together. She couldn't imagine any desire to continue plunging through life, killing everything in her path. Plants, animals, insects, oceans.

Doors were opening. Trap doors were opening, too, and she was falling through, spinning. She wanted to fly out of her mind through the spinning triangles into the Nevermind, the place where nothing real happened, only sweet stories about Emily.

She wanted to get away, cross her eyes, dissociate, move sideways into a colorful land. Who doesn't want to escape into lovely when considering culpability? Seeing themselves for all they are in the mirror. The desire to look away is the obstacle to a better world.

She washed the dishes, the warm water and ugly gunk of scrambled eggs pushing up rubbery and slimy against her fingers. She felt very strange. All the childlike wonder in her life was draining away. All the playfulness and creativity. She felt leaden. Colors seemed dusty. Sound was boring.

And Julio. She didn't get why she cared. He was nice, but who gave a fuck about sex, anyway? Messy and nasty. Smelly.

And so were people. She would just break into the church and get the XXX and kill off as much of humanity as she could. But no, she didn't remember that weird word she had to use to open the door. That was like some other part of herself that was dying.

Parts of her were going away, and as they did, what was left had less of their memories. Ah, but she had the recording of the key to the poison room. A little bit wouldn't be missed.

People's lives were not worth remembering anyway. Flat. Gray. Safe. She had no desire to contact Brandon again. Who cared? The more people died from poisoning, the better. Fewer children and grandchildren to come after them and carry on the tradition of ruining the earth.

She wondered if fingernails had calories. She stared at the half-moons on hers. They were a poor substitute for a real moon rise. She raised her hand in the air and her arms fell listlessly to her side as she stared down at them in boredom with her own existence as a parasite on the earth.

She got a phone call and answered it. She didn't care if it was Geoff or not. If he killed her, who cared? She was only a vile human.

It wasn't quite 9:00 in the morning. She was offered the job at a bottling plant. *That's good. I couldn't possibly have gone to work anymore. I'm done with that damn job. I never want to see Geoff again until he's in custody.*

She imagined taking it and dropping XXX in at the last stage after the water was cleaned and was ready to be bottled. Countless people would drink it and die. Give the animals a fighting chance. It sounded like a better idea moment by moment.

"I'll think on it and tell you later today. During business hours." She didn't mind saying it with a rude tone of voice to the nice lady on the phone. In fact, she kind of liked it.

The phone rang and she took the chance. The manager said, "I'm sorry to inform you, Nancy. Martha was found dead in her apartment. There's no sign of struggle, so we're hoping she didn't suffer."

Nancy worked hard to care. She only worried about whether Martha's pet snake would be set free in a good forest.

CHAPTER TWENTY-TWO
Trio

She'd promised her piano teacher she would try for a breakthrough every day. "The further away you are from yourself," he had said, "the more you need to practice that day, not less. To play like a master you have to feel intensely, love and guilt, redemption and revenge." It was well into Friday and she hadn't opened the piano lid. The last thing she knew how to do at that moment was feel. Anything. But, she would keep the promise. She was paying for the lessons after all, and money was money.

She flexed her muscles and slapped her cheeks. She felt hollow. She jumped up and down, waved her arms around, and breathed fast, trying to feel excitement. *Where are you, me? Come to Mama.*

She sat down to play, beginning the song she wrote when young. She played it with her right hand as usual. And then, her left hand naturally began a complementary part. She recognized it: the song when Dog jumped out of the box.

She marveled over how she hadn't remembered that a song played when the box opened, until she was at the church with Julio. But now, with her fingers on the keys, it came back full force, and she understood: that was why her song seemed so thin. There was more to the song that haunted her than just the one part. And that song that Dog played was the second melody that she'd been searching for since her youth. A missing component of the music that let in the compartmentalized part. She felt filled in. She was in color.

The song she played was like the Schoenberg three-part piece for the piano, in which the motifs were combined among them, made of three notes. But, what was the third note, the third part of herself? It felt dissonant with only those two parts. More evocative and full, but not enough. Not enough! Where was the rest of her?

She stood up. It felt as if the rest of herself was in the room with her. And the parts of her whole self teamed up.

Her heart's rhythms no longer felt distant. Her voice lowered as she sang. She felt the *duende*.

She strode to the drawer where she kept the smut and opened it without hesitation.

There *was* no smut. There were no books, no magazines. Only clothing and memories of something real. A black dress in dire need of washing, soaked with gin, tobacco, cologne, semen, with a sticky sucker stuck to it. Next to it were knee socks and a child's necklace, beside condoms and black mesh underwear. Sharp wire and a handgun. Recording devices and notes in different handwriting.

She suddenly heard the complete tune in her head she had written when she was young. She remembered the third part, at the same time she was remembering having been programmed to forget it. A song, wailing, tragic, distant, coming closer. Power. The salvation of the rest of herself.

She ran back to the piano. She played, the music taking her over. All three parts.

The part she'd always remembered, as Nancy.

The other part that Dog played.

And the third part, lower notes, complex chords.

She gave it all heart and intensity that made her whole body feel as if the blood were rushing through in ways it had not since she first wrote the song. Sensuous and passionate. No wonder people had praised her for being a child prodigy, predicting she'd win a scholarship to Juilliard and perform for the masses. She had been brilliant.

And she was brilliant again.

She was fully Emily. Fully Angela Ageless. Fully Nancy. She fully integrated. She cared again. *Who doesn't have trouble embracing all the parts of herself? Just in time. Two of me almost died.*

The music swelled, as she played flamboyantly, her arms going wild, as she threw her body around to the fast, complicated music, singing out with a deep throaty voice full of poignancy, pushing the pedals, attacking the keys with fervor. The crescendo shook the apartment, rattled the windows, and she was free.

She got it.

A little of the XXX was going to snake handling churches, to use when they felt the anointing of the Lord.

Some money was allocated to murder people the agencies wanted to get rid of, such as the most vocal student activists staging protests against foreign policy.

The evangelists gathered information about countries the U.S. wanted to take down. Through their network of churches, they would deliver the undetectable poison, and it would be used to assassinate the countries' leaders and their supporters. In their places, dictators trained by the agencies would be brought into power. She had helped with that training. She was a key component of the Joint Operations. She was a skilled cleaner.

She had *killed* Rios.

The poor man had been taken from a good life in his home country and told he would be able to make a lot of money playing football, and he could support his family and charities and even his President. She had been involved in throwing football games Geoff bet on to fund the Nevermind's psyops.

She ran to the computer, looking up everything she had just realized. Suspicious key words be damned. She was at it for an hour, putting the pieces together. Her fingers kept flying across the keys. Her brain was working doubletime. Figuring it out took tremendous focus and clever strategies to bypass programming.

She saw the Nevermind's agenda from their point of view. Geoff wasn't sadistic, but serving the policy of his country. He was a patriotic spy. But, at what cost?

Every time an image of flying on Bennu out the window came up to block her memories, she rubbed the toes of one foot over the toes of the other one. Somehow that diverted her attention. She would pinch herself as she started to trance. She drank coffee to stay alert and not fall into the Nevermind states of numbness, euphoria, delusion or bewilderment. She fought her way through the funhouse, breaking the mirrors.

She turned the funhouse upside down, and the shards of reflection fell to the floor. She put the pieces together again, but not the same way. This time, she was in control, and they pieced together an entirely different picture.

She paced and sang the song she'd remembered from youth, the three parts. She danced in front of the triptych of ancient pianists.

She had taken down countries; the Agency believed the ends justified the means. She had relayed encoded information across continents. Could she turn the tables without betraying government secrets? She'd been involved in instigating coups. No wonder she'd been warned so many times. The Agency needed her. She maintained the status quo of the United States and its allies.

Tantra Bensko

She'd poisoned Martha.

She'd done the job they'd given her. They'd given her no choice. Now, she had a choice.

It was time to face her monster.

Nancy thrilled that the pills were finally gone from her system. She celebrated how she'd remembered the piano piece in time to save her compartmentalized selves from self-destructing when the last chemical molecules flushed away. Nancy was ready for action. She'd contact Brandon and...

All the muscles in her body tightened. Her stomach leapt inside her tummy. The Jollys! She would have run out the night before, if she'd been taking them regularly. She couldn't let Geoff suspect that she had any memories returning. How could she smile and act like he was just her uncle and boss, after all she'd been through in the last two weeks?

No. Yes. She had seen him. She'd been seeing him *regularly* all along. As Emily, and as Angela. He was their goddamn ride.

The memories burst through her consciousness and she could almost smell him close by; his stinky body in the clothes he wore too long, his unclean diet oozing through his pores, his greasy hair sticking up in dirty-blond curls, his stubble which he pressed against her like sandpaper, his dark glasses, so sharp and black and close to her face, the lenses thick. His bald spot she looked down on when he laced her long black boots before he took her for a ride or when he took them off and changed them into pink slippers.

Sometimes Geoff was with Crank as well. She remembered them standing in the private bar in the back of the church, bent toward each other laughing, their big bellies shaking in the dim light, rows of bottles behind them on the shelves. And she just a polite, quiet little girl, worrying if they'd wreck on the drive... a strawberry blond girl being

208

taught the Rosicrucian Enochian method for becoming more than human.

The feel of her fingers against the filmy, granular feel of a dress. Moving it between her fingers, hearing the scratchy sound it made. How she liked to look through the gauze hanging down in the secret room, the candlelight flickering golden behind it, making such subtle shadows moving across the paper and the glinting chains.

Then the memory came of Crank shouting Enochian at her when she'd gotten a code wrong that she was practicing, his flat red face close to hers, his gray jowls shaking. She'd sat with him in the secret room, and they'd practiced the codes for each paper spy doll hanging down, spinning around. She'd loved getting it right almost every time, being so smart with such a perfect memory, always obedient, the magical moonchild of the apocalypse. The heroine of the movie that would be shown in the theaters soon — unless she changed the plot. It could be an embarrassment if some kind of stink was happening that the public would pay attention to if the movie came out.

Or maybe the movie *should* come out. Then the stink would get people's attention. People who got a clue would be turning other people on to Brandon's videos by the droves.

She was impressed with herself. The Enochian code signals Emily had memorized were complex, all right angle turns, a tiny labyrinth on a board, on a football field, on the theatrics of the stage, on the sacrifice of countries. She was similar to the football coach, bending down, giving pregame signals of the plays to the players bent and huddled intently around him. No, she was like the umpire. And she was a cutie in polka dot tights.

Sometimes, she was with Martha. Swaying their hips together. Practicing sliding their hands up and down bananas. Drinking cocktails and laughing.

Sometimes, she was even with Bennu. No, not Bennu exactly: that was the product of the famous Nevermind hypnosis. She was with *Jeff...* Jeff handing her her black thong underwear with his flamingo hook with the big bird eyes, dangling them in front of her face, the sharp point directed at her, only an inch from her own eyes. She remembered too: there were cameras in those flamingo eyes. DARPA creations that had far more advanced functions than just recording. Controlling.

She remembered Jeff twisting his hand sewn on in reverse, the index finger being where the pinkie was, the palm palm-forward. The motion of turning it back and forth, back and forth, brought up the star of the pulsation between the upward and the downward pointing triangles, the Sign of Solomon, which went spinning to the right. She'd suddenly become Emily. To the left and she'd be back to Nancy, as if nothing had happened.

As she remembered, she resisted the personality switch. The depth of the song she had written before she was dazed by the explosion had broken the spell of staying on the surface.

She couldn't childishly pretend nothing evil was going on. She couldn't justify her job with necessary patriotism anymore.

She remembered the times when she and Jeff had been children and had been allowed gentle baths together to bond. Geoff had poured the warm water all over her using a bucket. The candles around the tub had reflected in the mirrors, but she hadn't cared. Her eyes and her mind were completely inside him as she cared about him, him as a person, like a brother. She had let her fingers press his arm with gentle

210

reverence. Her touch was at once light and deep, trembling and firm. She looked into his eyes. His thin lips raised into a bit of a smile, and so did hers. He touched her back with his hand that was still on straight. They held hands and were quiet, not playing or washing, just being with each other.

And his father coming in, grabbing him by the wrists, holding his hands in front of her nose and saying to her, "Take a last look, chica." The man let the delicate skin turn red as he twisted the boy's wrists. He pulled him out of the house. There was the bang in the night. Then, he delivered the hands to her and set them into the water.

It was going to be over soon. She would escape the Nevermind. She wouldn't likely be tried for her work on the coup, drug-running, assassination, entrapment and passing secrets. That would endanger national security. Intelligence was above the law, and such actions were matter-of-course. They were expected. That's what made the country run. Would people really give up all that kept them secure in their beds, accruing money from their investments that relied on what she did? If she tried to out any of the Agents, other than the ones already ambiguously outed, like Crank, it would be disastrous legally, too.

She had some loyalty to the Nevermind's cause. A lot of hogwash occult, hypnosis and propaganda. All for what? To lull the nation. To get away with murder. She was a serial killer for the country.

She was not just Nancy. Just as well; that nihilist might have made short work of hordes of people through the bottling plant. Or maybe she'd only fantasize about it whenever she felt the horrors over all the trash she threw away.

But, she had to impersonate being only Nancy, naive and idealistic. And she had to ask Geoff for another bottle of pills. He had to know she'd gone without the pill that day.

She had to come up with a story. With new memories flooding in, it would be like hanging out with a boss while secretly on LSD. Really, it was hanging out with the boss without revealing she knew he'd given her LSD as a child. The world reconfigured itself anew.

But first, she emailed Brandon. "I was programmed with an Ehroh movie along with Helen, the woman who wrote a book implicating Crank. I haven't read it; I don't want to be influenced, anyway. Another movie is being made now, and it will be used to program more children. It's magickal. Has occult power and messages. And it's fucking based on me. I want to keep it from coming out, though. I think."

She waited. Would he answer? For ten minutes, she got up and drank water, stretched, checked the computer compulsively.

Finally, he responded. "We'll see what we can do."

"What do you think will happen to me?"

"You've got to go to a good cobbler for your bona fides. Pick a new cover you'll like, but don't get too attached to it. Be ready to change fast. The women survived who put out the books implicating Crank in fomenting coups using mind control patsies. They didn't get killed, even though they claimed that their personalities were split into different compartments and forced to be mass murderers for the other programs. Churches, military, secret society, Aryan supremacy. Occult groups. There are conferences about it, books, magazines, therapists. Lots of HUMINT, too. But watch out, because most of what you read about it is disinformation. It's a labyrinth of deception, and finding out the truth is almost impossible."

She wrote, "I can't even imagine how anyone learned how to make people dissociate."

"The Nazi Paperclip doctors brought the techniques to the U.S. Brilliant psychopaths, eh?"

"What techniques?" she asked.

"Assassin programming, using Dissociative Identify Disorder through trauma. Manchurian Candidate stuff. Vacaville. Personality Modification. Read about it."

She bit her fingers, making her falter as she typed: "Right now, I have imperfect memories that come and go. I plan to gather evidence. I need redemption for my crimes. Please help disseminate this to the public when the time is right."

"You don't want it out now?"

"I don't know. Maybe decide what you think. I don't want to release sensitive information that would cause a problem for our economy without having a backup plan about how to stabilize the country. I'll do analysis."

"That's wise, Nancy."

"Or make me an insurance plan like yours. I can pay. Without it set up to go public, everything I'm learning would be useless if I die before it gets out. It's legal for me to assassinate people for the government. But, to turn my back on my job, and turn in my Nevermind bosses, no, it's not."

"You assassinated people?"

"I'm Nevermind."

There was no return message. When she sent him another message, it was returned as blocked. She gasped and covered her face with her hands. What would she do if he pulled out?

Her connection went down. She pulled out the router, waited thirty long seconds and reconnected it. Nada.

Then she remembered more. The real message she needed to get to Brandon. And the ticking clock she had to beat. She remembered what the metal boxes in the tiny room were. They had the Enochian locks on them. Inside them were Bibles with their insides cut out. Inside *them* were indestructible metal containers containing XXX.

She called Brandon on the phone. She realized he didn't know her number, so maybe he wouldn't block her if she launched in without identifying herself. He picked up. There was no sound but his voice run through a distortion device, automated: "You are being recorded. State your name and address. Do not use my name in our conversations. Do not say anything you are not willing to be heard by the NSA."

She blurted out, "Some of the XXX will be shipped overseas on Terry Crank's plane inside Bibles sent to evangelists working with the Nevermind tomorrow. Can you help me stop it tonight? I don't know how yet."

Silence. He hung up.

She called again. He didn't answer.

This was her mission. She'd finally solved the mystery and figured out her part in it and how to stop it, and Mr. Tough Guy was too scared to follow through. Fuck! Alyssa idolized a wuss. Nancy wouldn't even get a chance to show off to her that she was the one ready for activism. She kicked and punched the air.

She tried calling Geoff to tell him she was coming by to get the pills, but the phone went dead. She put it back down and picked it up again. No dial tone. She checked the cord and jiggled it.

Geoff put her to work whenever he had the chance. It was time to take the Bibles she had filled with XXX to Crank's airport under the added cover of darkness, so when everything was all set and he and his crew could take off first thing in the morning without a hitch.

On the way to Geoff's house she stopped at a pay phone and called Brandon.

"Can you help me or not?"

He didn't hang up. Instead, he said, "Crank is Nevermind as far as I can tell. He has immunity to do whatever he wants. So, what can you do?"

She said, "I'm gathering what I can, pointing to behavior among the Nevermind that might be considered beyond the call of duty. They can only cover it up so much if the public gets wind of it and there's evidence presented on the nightly news as well as on your channel, right?"

His voice was low. "Always a crap shoot."

She stated, "I'm going to Geoff's house before it gets too late and he comes here. I don't have a cell phone. I won't have access to the internet. But, I'll contact you if I can. If I can't get ahold of you, these messages are going to look bad tomorrow."

Meanwhile, she was preparing her window dressing, like packing her favorite goofy comic book into her purse, covering up the gadgets underneath.

"This is getting interesting,"she thought to herself.

CHAPTER TWENTY-THREE
Biblegeddon

Nancy remembered Angela had a high tech tiny recording device in the drawer. It was shaped like a short fat pen. Nancy stuck it in her pocket next to the flash drive. She made a variety of recordings, on different devices, of Enochian tones that unlocked the thick metal XXX containers that went inside the Bibles, unlocked the Bibles, and also the boxes they were in. She left twenty minutes of blank time at the beginning of the recordings.

The evangelists associated with the embassy, who were to receive them and open them, had to be high-voiced women as well. She marveled at how much thought went into orchestrating the coup.

She drove to Geoff's house. Seeing it with fresh eyes brought back memories of living there as a teen. So many parts of the house she was not allowed into, so many trunks locked and closets emanating strange smells.

When he answered the door, he said, "I expected to hear from you earlier. You OK? I was about to come get you in a little bit. Your phone connection dead for some reason? I hear you've been taking more days off than usual... I mean, really OK? None of those pesky mental issues when you forget to take your medicine?"

The number of questions flustered her, and she had to hold onto her identity to keep from spinning. "I'm OK, just a case of food poisoning I think. I forgot all about the pills running out. You know, with so many in all the emergency places, it's hard to keep track. Sure, I had some woozy hallucinations, but probably just from bad fish, you know? I'm getting better."

Does he have access to my Smart Meter readings? They'd tell him what appliances I was using. He'd know I was lying about lying around being sick. Was that why things went dead? The Agents knew I was about to spill the beans?

He put his hand on her back and ushered her in gently. "Well, no harm done. I'm glad you're recovering nicely. I'm sure since you're behind on the pills you'll want to go ahead and take one now without waiting until the usual hour."

"Oh no, that's OK. I don't want to screw up the schedule. You know how then I have to take a Jolly an hour later every day until the timing normalizes again. I don't want to bother with that."

"Yes, you do. You know how you get if you don't take them for a day, much less a day and a half. Come now. I'll go get the bottle upstairs."

She grabbed his cell phone from his jacket pocket and called Brandon. She whispered, "Are you free to be on standby for a few hours? Scrupulous dry cleaning recommended on this one." She couldn't believe she was doing this, leaving a record on his phone of the outgoing call in case he ever thought to check it. But, if she had her way, it wouldn't matter soon. He'd be under arrest.

He said, "Yes."

"Got a car ready with the gas tank filled up and your fleet ready to go with you on a chase?"

"Yes, good." His voice was fast as if he wasn't wasting time to pause between words.

"There are boxes of Bibles addressed to three evangelists connected with the embassy, who are to dump them in the water supply. The evangelists know the Enochian key to open the Bibles. Perfect way of protecting them from prying eyes, no? I can deliver Ears Only information with twisty Enochian, too."

"You know this? It's not a false memory from an overactive imagination?" Brandon's voice was growing more intense, almost pointy.

"A different alter knew all the details and arranged the plane. But, I've integrated completely now, so that alter can't hurt you."

Silence.

She said, "I suspect we'll be driving there within three hours in a truck. I don't know what the truck will be like yet, but I'll try to let you know, so you can follow us. Can you arrange a wreck?" She was aware of how bold her own voice sounded. More than most women's voices could become. She kind of liked that.

"A wreck?"

She explained: "One that won't hurt other motorists. So the little road to the airport is our marker. Hardly anyone drives on that. We're working naked, so you shouldn't need much of a fleet. I'll unlock the Bibles and the metal boxes they're in, and I hope to fucking God it's possible to unlock the back of the truck. I want the Bibles to land on the road and open and spill the containers inside for all the world to see the deception."

"But how, if no one drives there?"

"It's got to be covered by the press. Can you contact them, so they'll be there in time?" She could hardly wait to hear his answer.

A creak on wood. Geoff was coming down the stairs. There was so much more to say. But, she disconnected and slipped his phone back into his jacket pocket.

The feel of the cell leaving her hand in such haste brought back a body-memory. As Angela, she had a cell phone with all the up-to-date technology built in. Nancy could have been using that if she'd dug far enough into the drawer. But, there was no going back to get it now. How would she contact Brandon to let him know the make and license plate of the truck?

Geoff said, "So, I have to do everything? Sink's over here, in case you forgot, missy." He filled up a glass with water from the jug in the refrigerator and put ice in it. He handed her the bottle and put one pill in her hand. "It's a good thing these kick in so fast. Or do you want to take extra to celebrate seeing me again? Fun times, eh, chickiepoo? It's been three weeks."

"They're not so fun, really. The pills hardly do anything for me anymore." She whined like a spoiled brat.

"Well, I do a lot for you in case you haven't noticed. What? You don't appreciate me giving them to you for free? Maybe I should start charging you. And for back payment we can start from the time you were a child and first diagnosed with paranoid delusions? No, that would be unfair. Your father should have been paying for medication for you then, but he didn't believe it. He wasn't. You know why?"

"No."

"Because he was not the smartest man in the world, was he, little one? He didn't really think you needed medication when you were little. And then, he actually even started to believe your delusions when anyone could see you were being a silly willy-nilly. Can you imagine? So, sure I went along with it. No anti-psychotic meds. But, these little babies do the trick, don't they? Still labeled experimental after all this time, because so few people have the disease they're for, but hell, they sure sell well on the street. You can't tell me they're not nice. Can you, now? Hmm?" He patted her on the head and she pushed his hand off. "What, why so feisty today, chica? What, what, what?" He squeezed her cheek.

"How old was I when he started to believe me?"

"I'd say around sixteen." He leaned in closer. His breath smelled like shit. "Wouldn't you?"

She pretended to put the pill in her mouth and then drank a sip.

"You missed a little something," he said. He took her hand in his and uncurled her fingers. "Look. You forgot!" He put it in her mouth. "Drink up. There's a good girl. Now open wide and let me see."

She didn't want to arouse any more suspicion by hiding it under her tongue. She hoped against hope he hadn't realized what she'd been up to. It dissolved too quickly for her to be able to remove it without him seeing it. She had to swallow before opening her mouth, her face reddening. She wanted to bite down on his fingers when he pulled her mouth apart. This would be a test of her psychological integration.

If the authenticity wasn't 100 percent complete, she wouldn't be impersonating Emily soon. She would really become her. She'd have no idea what the XXX in the Bibles was going to be used for, no thought about unlocking them so they'd fall onto the ground in a wreck and open up for all to see.

This was her big chance to bring the evangelical involvement in the coup to public light. Simply reporting it to the police would do nothing. It had to be reported in a format people could download and keep forever.

Maybe an independent TV news station would include it on the midnight news if it wasn't policed by a CIA

Nevermind propaganda liaison. The station wouldn't have time to look at it closely enough but would just run it fast, excited about a big sensation and more views.

She hoped Brandon had contacts with independent stringers. They'd be all over a bizarre wreck like that. If they gave it to the station without showing the small labels on the metal boxes containing the Bibles indicating the evangelist contact at the embassy, maybe it would slip through and that part could come out later in his videos.

Geoff asked, "Are you hungry? I was about to eat a late dinner. Or don't you like taking food from me either, all of a sudden?"

"Sure. It smells good." She'd rather eat in silence than come up with conversation until the time for her Emily act to begin.

"Set the table, honey?"

So she did. The knife in her hand made her want to stab him, but revenge wasn't in her nature. Redemption was. Justice. And stopping the crime of poison she was implicated in. He glanced up at her as she stood by the table, knife in hand, looking at him. She put it down by the plate.

He served a roast with potatoes and carrots, though she said, "I try not to eat meat anymore, uncle. Poor animals and all that, you know."

"Oh, come off it. Just eat it. It's good for you."

She ate in silence, estimating the time the pills took to kick in and then took on a more facile expression, as if she lived on the surface of a colorful bubble floating through the sky. She concentrated on her attraction to Julio in order to make her pupils dilate appropriately.

When dinner was over, Geoff said, "There's something I want to show you in your old room." That phrase reminded her she had heard it over and over and over during the years. She'd blanked out each time she heard that trigger phrase.

221

She faked an empty look this time and followed him upstairs and entered the room she'd lived in from sixteen to nineteen. It had trunks with her favorite childhood dresses and toys.

"Look at this," he said, bending down to the toy chest and lifting up a square tin box, flipping the tiny lever so the lid opened, and a dog's head popped out on a spring. The perfect replica of Dog. Just a little dirty and ragged. The music it played when it was wound up was the same: the element of the song that had made her integrate when she'd listened to it with Julio, in a state of openness. She pretended not to hear the song as she stood next to Geoff, and gave the impression that she shifted fully into her little girl personality.

"Time to get dressed now, sweet little Emily. Here, I'll help you." She didn't want to leave her recording and her recording devices there.

She spoke in a high voice and curtseyed, saying, "Can I wear an adult dress today, and carry a purse? And wear lipstick and eye shadow? I want to play dress-up." She hoped she was getting the pouty, pleading, yet self-assured child voice just right. A slight mistake could cost her life.

He hesitated, his eyes studying her face. She passed gas and giggled.

He looked convinced. "Sure, sure, that's easier anyway. Close your eyes, and clap your hands three times. Then run and look in the mirror."

She did, and laughed, pretending excitement at seeing herself in adult clothes with a purse.

She was glad she'd become authentic and taken the chance of combining all her selves, so the Jolly had no effect this time. She wished she could show her uncle she actually was capable of putting the pieces together.

He got out her child's makeup kit from the trunk and applied it, somewhat sloppily. "Your mouth is trembling, stop that. You're making me color outside the lines. And we always color inside the lines, right, sweetie?"

"Always perfectation!"

He chuckled. "That's right. Perfection eternal. Let's get to work. You like work, don't you? You're so good at it. And today there is very little to do. You just need to go with me to get the boxes of Bibles and take them to Terry's airport. If you're good, you can go up on his plane next time he's in town, OK? Won't that be fun? You can fly!"

"I love to fly. Flying's my favorite. Even Bennu is nice when we fly." She ran around the room in circles flapping her arms and skipping, leaping up on one foot like a ballet dancer and spinning around.

"Well, let's head to the Divine Rays then, shall we, pretty?" He took her by the hand, and they went out to his car. As he drove, she pretended to sleep. Less pretense required. Being an imposter was exhausting.

They arrived at the empty church. He pulled a loading cart from the storage room down the hallway, and she intoned to open the secret door. They went inside. Then came the hard part. "Do you want me to help you today or do you want to do it yourself?"

"Myself! I'm getting good at it. Want to watch?" Nancy kept her expression wide-eyed and innocent as she pulled down her panties. She pretended to give herself an infantile, naive orgasm quickly. She then intoned the Enochian words required to open the second door, trying to hide the shame reddening her cheeks. *You'll pay for traumatizing me as a child to split my personality, even if you were doing it on orders from the government! No Intelligence operation is important enough to make a child alter do that. Especially when the operation's based on greed.*

He said, "I won't fit in there until we get some of the boxes out of the way. Can you hand me some?"

She squeezed inside the room and passed him the heavy metal boxes containing many Bibles each, and he put them on the cart. He carried one cartload after another out to what she assumed was a truck waiting in the parking lot. "Can I ride on the cart? I want to, I want to!"

"OK, if you help me put the boxes in the truck." He lifted her on top of the boxes and pushed the cart extra quickly, making her laugh, her skirt flying up from the breeze.

She held her arms out as she rode and touched the wall with her right hand all the way. As her hand passed by the thermostat, she raised the tiny lever so the heat in that part of the building would rise.

She couldn't keep up the laughter when she saw the truck. It was the same waste management truck that she had chased before! She shivered. She memorized the license plate. The driver was not around. She hoped Geoff was driving and there was no one else or there was instead a different driver. She really didn't want to see the same driver as before. What would she do?

Would he recognize her as the woman he'd avoided in the long chase two weeks before? Did he know who she was and what role she played as a secret Agent of the Nevermind? Was he a contractor?

They went back in for more boxes. She reasoned that the driver must be involved or Geoff wouldn't casually leave the door to the secret rooms open when he was in the vicinity. She knew Geoff with his deep voice couldn't make the sound necessary to get in. The code changed every week as an added protection.

It was set to change at midnight. The unlocking sound for the boxes and the Bibles changed with it. If their process got slowed up, her recording wouldn't work as planned, the wreck would have no purpose, and the XXX would end up in the hands of the evangelists and in the entire water supply

224

where the dear President was already struggling against the false charges of homosexuality.

Rios was being presented as a loser who died from a drug overdose. The deaths from the water were to be blamed on his President's new free water system. It had to look flawed.

"I guess I'm getting old," Geoff said. "All this exercise is making me overheat." He took off his jacket and laid it down. When he took the next cartload of boxes to the truck, Nancy grabbed his phone from the pocket and called Brandon.

She described the waste management truck in detail and told him the approximate time to expect them to be on the road to the private airport. "The back of the truck has an easy latch to leave unlocked if I can manage to get back and do it right before we leave without the driver seeing us. If I can't do that, the plan is worthless. But, believe me, flaps and seals are my specialties."

"You're prepared for whatever might happen to you?"

"Yes. I don't think the police will come after me any more than they would go after you, in spite of the heavy footprint."

"For different reasons, of course." Well, if Alyssa ever found out what she had done, maybe she'd put her on a par with that know-it-all. Nancy was proud of what she was doing. But, she wasn't about to go bragging about it in a one-upmanship game like Brandon did.

"The waste truck has to turn over."

"Got it."

"Can you let some stringers know about the wreck? I guess it would look fishy if you told them about it ahead of time, but I'd love to see the news there immediately."

"I'll use a different name and call in a false alert for a robbery at a location nearby. Then, if the wreck happens, I'll call it in for real, and they'll be there in a hot minute."

"Be careful. I don't want to see you or your fleet get hurt."

"What about you?"

"I don't care. Even if I die, the evidence speaks for itself."

"Salute."

"Salute."

She put Geoff's phone back, ran down the hall to lower the temperature and back into the poison room, which was no longer small but had become spacious.

There were still many cans of XXX and a variety of delivery methods, containers and additives. But, the boxes of Bibles were nearly gone. One more load to go. The time was getting very close.

The unlocking tone would change soon, and if the boxes fell onto the road, they wouldn't open, so the event would be nothing newsworthy. There was nothing she could do to hurry up the process, so she just breathed faster as if time would slow down if she could outrun it. She sweated more from time than from heat.

Yet, she put on her protective gear that made her look like the Bee of Ra. She put her purse over her shoulder, adding to the bizarre effect. When Geoff returned, she said, "Dress-up day! I want to wear *this* on the trip!"

He chuckled and agreed. "OK, cutie. Why the hell not?" He loaded the last of the boxes on the cart, and she toned to lock the inner and outer doors. As they went down the hallway to the truck, he made a phone call. "Ready, Max. Any time you are."

She reached into the back of the truck to straighten the boxes and lodged the small recording of the unlocking tone behind some boxes. Assuming they left the parking lot in time before the men heard the Enochian, the tones would unlock everything inside. The unlocked boxes and Bibles

226

would spill their contents during the wreck while keeping the XXX containers closed until someone twisted their latches and opened them. The sound wouldn't travel to the front of the truck.

But, she realized, whoever opened them needed to be warned. She had to write a note. She searched the parking lot quickly and found a scrap of dirty paper. She searched for a pen and found nothing. She tried writing with a charred piece of wood, but it was too moist. She picked up a tiny red chalky pebble and tried, but it barely made a mark. She picked up a page from a book and scanned it for an appropriate warning word to tear out, but there wasn't one. Her vision became blurry from trying to read so fast in such a panic.

As Geoff lifted the last of the boxes onto the truck, she saw a shadow coming around the corner. It was indeed the same driver as before. She curtseyed. He grinned but didn't show any signs of recognition. How could he, with her face covered with the protective goggles and face mask on top of that?

She struck up a chatty conversation with him and watched as he brought down the back of the truck. Perfect. It would stay closed until the wreck, but nothing kept it from opening under impact.

Then, he took out a padlock. She gasped. How would she obtain the key in time?

When he turned the lock around, she saw it was a combination lock. The plan was falling apart.

They stood by the back of the truck as Geoff and Max talked. Time was running out. They'd hear the tones if they were standing there.

She took off her ring and stuck it in her pocket. "Can I get in the back of the truck for a minute? I realized I left something in there. My ring."

She stood close to him and watched out of her peripheral vision, memorizing the numbers as he unlocked it. Once he locked it back, they talked some more, and she sweated more under the protective layers. Finally, it was time to get in the truck. Max got in, and she said, "Oh, I have to pee first. I'll be right back."

She went to the back of the truck and squatted down behind it. As she did, she unlocked it and put the padlock in her pocket.

She hopped into the truck next to Geoff, and they were off.

She positioned herself so she could see the rear view mirror. Nothing unusual was happening on the major roads.

Then, as they got closer, she began to see black cars with blackened windows and windshields coming into view behind her in the distance, one at a time. The four cars followed them at a normal pace and distance, though they eased up a little closer to the turn off onto the long lonely road to the tiny private airport. Then, the cars approached behind them at an unprecedented speed. She held on and held her breath as if that would protect her.

Max looked into the mirror and hit the accelerator, throwing Nancy's head against the seat. "Fucktards. What the hell are they doing? Hold on."

The fleet chased them, gaining on them. One car pulled around and drove in front, at the same rate as Max. Mud covered the license plate entirely.

Another drove along the side, veering toward the waste management truck. Two drove behind. One nudged up close behind, fell back, then came closer again. Nancy's mask fogged up from her heavy breathing. She could barely make out what was happening on that dark night so away from streetlights. Beside them was a ditch. Perfect place for the truck to roll over and spill the Bibles. The wreck wouldn't endanger any traffic that might come along.

She was prepared to die. Max and Geoff were Agents too. Part of the job was the expectation to die for one's country. They'd signed on for it. To them, dying for their country meant taking down another one, using underhanded methods. They, no doubt, truly believed in their cause and were acting out of patriotism; she hoped they would survive.

She didn't want to be a murderer, but the point was to prevent a vast number of murders. To her, when going by her natural conscience, dying meant preventing whatever part of the coup she could.

But, she didn't look forward to the pain. The blood and gore. She wanted to live. To move on to another life on her own for the first time. To live as an authentic person. Free. Or if incarcerated, at least on her own terms. She was prepared for whatever the consequences were.

She quietly unlocked her seat belt and slipped it off stealthily as Max and Geoff argued, yelling. Geoff reached over to the steering wheel, and the truck veered back and forth.

She saw a speed bump ahead and registered that would be the ideal place for the wreck. Behind her, she saw the black car hang far back, honk and then zoom toward them. It was perfectly timed. Brandon was a pro.

She opened the door and jumped. She rolled down the ditch, feeling the bumps less due to the protective gear.

The black car roared up behind the truck, and before it smashed into it, the passenger door opened and a huge body flew out, rolling down in the ditch next to her. Brandon?

The other cars spread out. The car and the truck collided.

The truck arched over her in the moonlight, and she and the giant scrambled backward, trying to avoid the back of the truck landing on top of them, as the behemoth tilted and then crashed into the ditch.

The vehicle clamped down on the tip of her shoe, and she pulled her foot back, tearing off her shoe and wounding the tips of her toes. Boxes of Bibles spilled out on top of her and the giant, the sharp corners jabbing into whatever parts of their bodies were exposed. He was wearing protective gear as well, something like a mixture of Swat Team and motorcycle gangster.

The other cars screeched and honked, then two drove off into the night. "Come on," shouted the giant arising from underneath the boxes. "Brandon, here. Let's go!" He reached for her and pulled her up.

She could see less with each second as blood streamed into her eyes behind the goggles. She was dizzy as if wobbling on a tightrope above the scene. She couldn't move one arm, and one ankle didn't bend. He was limping too, holding his side, and bent over to wretch.

They scrambled up the side of the ditch with no solid foothold over slippery boxes sliding down. He really was tall.

He pulled the license plate off the back of the smashed black car. Smart. He must have been wearing huge gloves the whole time driving it, no fingerprints. His hands were disproportionally large. So were his feet. No doubt there was no discernible registration number. There was no way to trace it to him. And who could prove she was in the truck?

She took off her helmet and dabbed a finger into the blood. She wrote on the side of the inner wall of the truck near the back, dabbing again, writing more as her arm trembled. Finally, she finished writing, "XXX," to let them know it was poison and if they looked into it more, they'd realize exactly what poison it was.

Her DNA would be obvious on site. But she wasn't trying to get out of punishment. She'd turn herself in at the right time, without implicating anyone, with immunity if possible, and with the right evidence to incarcerate the criminals if a judge saw fit.

They jumped in the tall black car that was waiting and the driver pulled away, driving along at an ordinary speed into the darkness to the sound of multiple cars speeding to the scene. Brandon said, "The stringers will call an ambulance once they get their footage. They're going to love this. They'll get bonuses when the clips run on the midnight news. The newscasters will shit themselves when they find out what they've just shown. They'll never refer to it again."

She pulled off her protective gear, and he took off his huge helmet. His overgrown forehead was like a shelf sticking out over his eyes.

He added, "The major papers won't run it. But, little ones will. And the underground media will be on it like flies. Hurray, little lady, we did it!"

He shook her hand, which was completely enveloped by his. Then, he indicated the driver beside him. "We call this one Teddy Boy. He will be your driver for the evening. Would you like to enjoy a drink for your trip?" He handed her a water bottle, and she poured some on her sleeve and wiped the blood off her face where she'd been dabbing with a finger dirty from the truck. "Fancy a lift home? Teddy already knows where you live."

Teddy put his hand to his forehead and gave a little informal salute wave.

CHAPTER TWENTY-FOUR
Sharp

In the wee hours of the morning, the thick bush outside brushed up against Nancy's window. She was startled. *Just the wind. But, there is no wind. Just an animal. It would have to climb over the fence. But, there's that broken place in the fence.*

Whatever it was, it banged against the wall below. She was glad she was on the second floor and that the apartment's storage unit was underneath her. It made her feel a lot safer than being on the ground floor. Someone would have to climb the rose bush before it bent over and crashed from his weight onto the spikes of the agave cactus plants on each side. He'd have to scale the rest of the wall like a rock climber with good equipment.

Her heart felt as if it were splitting her ribs apart.

She could feel the red color of her blood, the mass of her heart, the urgency with which it wanted to survive.

CLINK!

Something thin and metallic caught onto the window ledge outside, like the hook an expert rock climber uses.

The sharp curved edge of it glinted.

She stared at it, only an inch long showing, like a curved stinger.

A pink hat with a curved bill rose up in her window, and below it, rising over the gray hair, a backward hand in a thick glove grasping onto the ledge, fingers tightly bent backwards to hold his weight.

Jeff's sparse eyebrows rose into her view, and then his straight eyelashes, then his eyes, blood-spidered around cold blue irises.

She ran the other way toward the phone, slipped on the floor, catching her foot as she scrambled, and searched for her landline under a pile of clothing.

Jeff's flamingo hook appeared in full, rearing back into space and whooshing forward suddenly, smashing the glass that shattered into her bedroom.

To the neighbors, it would just sound like someone throwing bottles around in the recycling bins as usual. She called out for help.

The metal hooked onto the inside of her wall with a grungy CLINK!

Jeff swung back and forth to knock out glass sticking up along the bottom of the window with his hook. He pulled himself up through the opening, shards cutting him and ripping his clothes as he rushed into her room, like a blur of shine and flash and red. His leg bled onto her floor.

She froze for a split second, then dodged him, throwing a pillow at him to gain time.

He raised up his arm, eyes fiercely glowering and leering at the same time, with a grin going up one side of his head. His hook aimed directly toward the welt in the center of her neck as if it were a target.

If she hadn't integrated her personalities, she wouldn't have known what to do. She would have been dead at that instant. Nancy was good at karate. But, Emily was a youthful fighting *machine*. And Angela owned a knife.

If the drawer she'd been avoiding before hadn't been open, Nancy couldn't have grabbed the knife in time. She reached under the clothing and pulled it out. The longest knife only a buff woman could wield.

She also pulled out an inch-high surveillance camera and clicked it on, setting it on the counter in the shadows, facing him. This would be the evidence she needed.

Nancy could do more than she thought she could, once she was all of herself. A hell of a lot more. As Jeff's hook came down within a fraction of an inch of her neck, she used moves on him far more deadly than anything taught in a family-friendly martial arts class. She kicked and punched, threw and jabbed, overpowering the bionic man and his sharp hook.

Jeff's hook slashed the couch, ripping it up completely, the foam inside flying through the air. He grazed her knee, knocking her backward, and she pretended that it mattered, as she was beyond pain, running on adrenalin. She went at it. Knife against hook.

Clink. Clink. CLINK!

She pinned him to the wall with her knife ready to enter his throat, his arm with the hook limp and bleeding from the slash clear across a tendon. He held his wrist with his reversed hand to slow the blood flow. He was helpless before her. She had won.

The police had been right about the poison not going to the dump. She'd take the risk. She'd trust them. She kept the knife at his throat while she reached over to her landline and dialed 911.

Then she remembered. The phone line was dead. She didn't want to let go of him while she went for her cell phone. She felt for his in his pocket and he grabbed it out of her hands and threw it out the window.

She screamed again as loudly as she could toward the window, "Call 911! I'm being attacked! Help, call the police! Murder!"

Jeff's body stank underneath her. Her own apartment matched the smell, as she hadn't been able to completely recover its pristine nature after her withdrawal period. Wafts of the stench hit them both at the same time as their expressions matched briefly, and then once again diverged.

She pushed against him and growled, her eyes fierce. There was hope. There was light at the end of her life, even if it was the light of her life flashing before her eyes at the moment of death. It would end with truth. It would end with honor. It would end with redemption.

Before long, the siren made Jeff tremble under her hands as his narrowed eyes glanced this way and that.

Even if she wouldn't be allowed to talk forthrightly in public, she'd have her say behind the scenes.

Since she'd broken through her split with the song, she could become free of the Nevermind. A woman worth hiring. A kick-ass woman no one would ever dare mess with. And a damn fine lay.

When the police knocked on the door, she let them in. They were three strapping men with guns ready to defend her. She stood tall, smiling at the officer's shock at the bloody scene, her clothes slashed most of the way off, her strawberry blonde hair wild as a banshee, foam covering the floor, wine bottles lined up along the counters, and a man with a flamingo for a hand *crying* in the fucking *corner*.

THE END

CHAPTER TWENTY-FIVE
About

The cover art is the "Fantastic Illustration Alice and Flamingo," by the wonderful artist, Annnmei.

The next book in the series is <u>*Remember to Recycle.*</u> Nancy's friend Becky, on the brink of a marriage proposal, becomes frightened when objects in her apartment are moved around when she's not there. She suspects that the man she loves, who films her during their BDSM sessions, is breaking in. Meanwhile, a homeless man she never pays any attention to as he digs through her recycling is not happy about the choices she's making.

All books in the <u>Agents of the Nevermind</u> series are Suspense with subcategories such as Conspiracy, Occult, Political and Spy Thrillers, Gothic Tale, Science Fantasy and Alternative History. Some characters recur in multiple books. Each book explores a different aspect of social engineering and the heroism of recognizing, resisting, and exposing it.

They take place in the same world as *Glossolalia*, which is basically this our own, but with this difference: the Agents of the Nevermind became part of the Intelligence community in the late 1980s, and the U.S. President ushering in the Occult Revival, making some changes to the society, as described in the Alternate History novel, *Giant Jack*, which is the prequel.

In the prequel, *Giant Jack*, in the 1980s and '90s, a scattered and hidden rural southern family finds a way to survive by medical subterfuge. Jack's yearnings take him from the alleyways of New Orleans through the circus to BLM land in California where a cult begins that changes the world. This novel is based on the real history of Human Growth Hormone as well as Theosophy as a function of espionage through hoaxes that led to the beliefs many people have today. The Agents manipulate the public through propagandistic popular media, mind control, and the occult.

Sign up for the newsletter at http://www.insubordinatebooks.com/ to learn the secrets behind these books, and consider "liking" the Tantra Bensko author page on Facebook and following on Twitter (TantraBensko).

Feel free to contact the author directly to discuss anything at mailto:flameflower@runbox.com.

And please be wonderful and review the books on Amazon! That would be fabulous! Go to the product detail page for the item on Amazon.com. Click Write a customer review in the Customer Reviews section. Click Submit.

Tantra Bensko teaches fiction writing with UCLA Extension Writing Program, Writers.com, Writers College, and Tantra Bensko's Online Writing Academy. She has an MA from FSU and an MFA from the University of Iowa Writers Workshop.

She has several other books of a Literary nature put out by a variety of publishers, two hundred stories and novelettes and nearly one hundred poems in magazines and anthologies. She has a website about the types of real-world topics addressed in the series called <u>The Engineering of Society.</u>

If you'd like to interview and/or invite her to do a guest blog post, please contact flameflower@runbox.com. If you write books about similar topics, fiction or non-fiction, and would like to bring your work to the attention of her audience, she's there to help. If you're passionate about the topics in this or other Nevermind books and want to talk about them or be interviewed in the blog, feel free.

If you like this book, you might also like the novels *Operation Mockingbird*, by Linda Balatsa, *Inside Out*, by Barry Eisler, and *The Orphan Trilogy*, by Lance and James Morcan.

Please review, be well, and enjoy life!

IB

Insubordinate Books
Berkeley, CA
http://www.insubordinatebooks.com/

sign up for the newsletter

for the rest of the books in
The Agents of the Nevermind
Series

recognize, resist, and expose propaganda

Made in the USA
Charleston, SC
27 January 2017